Dear Reader,

Looking back 

rd to realise that th ice I wrote my first *dam.* It wasn't until hat I found that onc ; was going to make had no intention of sending it to a publisher. It was my daughter who urged me to try my luck.

I shall never forget the thrill of having my first book accepted. A thrill I still get each time a new story is accepted. Writing to me is such a pleasure, and seeing a story unfolding on my old typewriter is like watching a film and wondering how it will end. Happily of course.

To have so many of my books re-published is such a delightful thing to happen and I can only hope that those who read them will share my pleasure in seeing them on the bookshelves again...and enjoy reading them.

Betty Neels

Back by Popular Demand

A collector's edition of favourite titles from one of the world's best-loved romance authors. Mills & Boon® are proud to bring back these sought after titles and present them as one cherished collection.

BETTY NEELS: COLLECTOR'S EDITION

101 A SUITABLE MATCH
102 THE MOST MARVELLOUS SUMMER
103 WEDDING BELLS FOR BEATRICE
104 DEAREST MARY JANE
105 ONLY BY CHANCE
106 DEAREST LOVE
107 THE BACHELOR'S WEDDING
108 FATE TAKES A HAND
109 THE RIGHT KIND OF GIRL
110 MARRYING MARY
111 A CHRISTMAS WISH
112 THE MISTLETOE KISS
113 A WINTER LOVE STORY
114 THE DAUGHTER OF THE MANOR
115 LOVE CAN WAIT
116 A KISS FOR JULIE
117 THE FORTUNES OF FRANCESCA
118 AN IDEAL WIFE
119 NANNY BY CHANCE
120 THE VICAR'S DAUGHTER

DISCOVERING DAISY

BY
BETTY NEELS

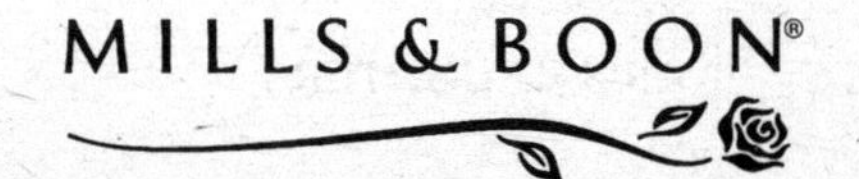

First published in Great Britain 1999 by Mills & Boon Limited
This edition 2001
Harlequin Mills & Boon Limited,
Eton House, 18-24 Paradise Road, Richmond, Surrey TW9 1SR

ISBN 0 263 82834 4

73-0801

Printed and bound in Spain
by Litografia Rosés S.A., Barcelona

CHAPTER ONE

IT WAS a blustery October afternoon and the dark skies had turned the sea to a dull grey, its sullen waves eddying to and fro on the deserted beach. Not quite deserted, for a girl was walking there, stopping now and again to stare seawards, stooping to pick up a stone and hurl it out to sea and then walk on again. She looked small and lonely with so much emptiness around her, and certainly she was both, but only because there was no one there to see.

She marched along at a furious pace, making no attempt to wipe away the tears; they didn't matter; they relieved her feelings. A good weep, she told herself, and everything would be over and done with. She would present a smiling face to the world and no one would be the wiser.

She turned back presently, wiped her eyes and blew her nose, tucked odds and ends of hair back under her headscarf, and assumed what she hoped was her normal cheerful expression. Climbing the steps back onto the sea front of the little town, she waved to the porter of the Grand Hotel across the road and started up the narrow, steep main street. The season was pretty well over and the town was settling down into its winter sloth; one could walk peacefully along its streets now, and chat unhurriedly with the shopkeepers, and the only cars were those of outlying farmers and the owners of the country properties dotted around the countryside.

There were narrow lanes leading off the street at intervals, and down one of these the girl turned, past a row of small shops converted from the old cottages which lined it; chic little boutiques, a jeweller's, a tiny tea room and, halfway down, a rather larger shop with a sign painted over its old-fashioned window: 'Thomas Gillard, Antiques'. The girl opened the door of the shop and the old-fashioned bell jangled.

'It's me,' she called ungrammatically, and pulled off her headscarf so that her nut-brown hair tumbled around her shoulders. She was an ordinary girl, of middle height, charmingly and unfashionably plump, her unassuming features redeemed from plainness by a pair of large hazel eyes, thickly fringed. She was dressed in a quilted jacket and tweed skirt, very suitable for the time of year but lacking any pretentions to fashion. There was no trace of her recent tears as she made her way carefully between the oak clap tables, Victorian Davenports, footstools and a variety of chairs: some very old, others Victorian button-backed balloon chairs.

Ranged round the walls were side cabinets, chiffoniers, and a beautiful bow-fronted glass cabinet, and wherever there was space there were china figurines, glass decanters and scent bottles, pottery figures and small silver objects. She was familiar with them all. At the back of the shop there was a half-open door leading to a small room her father used as his office, and then another door opening onto the staircase which led to the rooms above the shop.

She dropped a kiss on the bald patch on her father's head as she passed him at his desk, and went up the stairs to find her mother sitting by the gas fire in the sitting room, repairing the embroidery on a cushion cover. She looked up briefly and smiled.

'It's almost teatime, Daisy. Will you put the kettle on while I finish this? Did you enjoy your walk?'

'Very much. It's getting quite chilly, though, but so nice to have the town empty of visitors.'

'Is Desmond taking you out this evening, love?'

'We didn't arrange anything. He had to meet someone or other and wasn't sure how long he would be gone…'

'Far?'

'Plymouth…'

'Oh, well, he'll probably get back fairly early.'

Daisy agreed. 'I'll get the tea.'

She was fairly sure Desmond wouldn't come; they had gone out on the previous evening and had a meal at one of the town's restaurants. He had met some friends there. Being in love, she saw very little wrong with him, but some of his friends were a different matter; she had refused to go with them to a nightclub in Totnes and Desmond had been icily angry. He had called her a spoilsport, prudish. 'Time you grew up,' he had told her, with a nasty little laugh, and had taken her home in silence.

At the door he had watched her get out of the car and shot away, back to his friends, without saying another word. And Daisy, in love for the first time, had lain awake all night.

She had lost her heart to him when he had come into the shop, looking for glass goblets, and Daisy, being Daisy, twenty-four years old, plain, heartwhole and full of romantic ideas, had fallen instant prey to his superficial charm, bold good looks and flattering manners—all of which compensated for his lack of height. He was only a few inches taller than Daisy. He dressed well, but his hair was too long—sometimes, when Daisy allowed her sensible self to take over from romantic dreams, she did dislike that, but she was too much in love to say so.

He was a conceited man, and it was this conceit which had prompted him to invite Daisy out for dinner one evening, and that had led to more frequent meetings. He was a stranger to the little town, he had told her, sent by a London firm on a survey of some sort; he hadn't been explicit about it and Daisy had supposed him to be in some high-powered job in the City, and that had given him the excuse to get to know her.

She helped her father in the shop, but she was free to come and go, so that first dinner soon led him to being shown the town. His apparent interest in it had encouraged her to take him to the local museum, the various churches, the row of cottages leading from the quay, old and bowed down with history. He had been horribly bored, but her obvious wish to please him was food for his ego.

He'd taken her out to tea, plying her with witty talk, smiling at her over the table, and she'd listened to him egotistically talk about himself and his important job, laughing at his jokes, admiring a new tie, or the leather briefcase he always carried, so necessary to his image.

That he didn't care for her in the least didn't bother him; she served as a distraction in the dull little town after the life he'd lived in London. She was a stopgap until such time as he could find the girl he wanted; preferably with good looks and money. And a good dresser. Daisy's off-the-peg clothes earned her nothing but his secret mockery.

He didn't come that evening. Daisy stifled disappointment, and spent the hours until bedtime polishing some antique silver her father had bought that day. It was worn smooth by the years, and usage, and she thought how delightful it would be to eat one's food with such perfection. She polished the last spoon and laid it with the rest in a velvet bag, then put it in the wall cupboard where the small silver objects were housed. She locked the cupboard, shot the bolts on the shop door, locked it and set the alarm and went back upstairs. She had gone to the kitchen to make their evening drink when the phone rang.

It was Desmond, full of high spirits, apparently forgetful of their quarrel. 'I've a treat for you, Daisy. There's a dinner-dance at the Palace Hotel on Saturday evening. I've been invited and asked to bring a partner.' He turned on the charm. 'Say you'll come, darling, it's important to me. There'll be several people I've been hoping to meet; it's a good chance for me…'

When Daisy didn't speak, he added, 'It's rather a grand affair; you'll need a pretty dress—something striking so that people will turn round and look at us. Red—you can't ignore red…'

Daisy swallowed back excitement and happiness as she said sedately, 'It sounds very nice. I'd like to come with you. How long will it last?'

'Oh, the usual time, I suppose. Around midnight. I'll see you safely home, and I promise you it won't be too late.'

Daisy, who if she made a promise kept it, believed him.

Desmond said importantly, 'I'm tied up for the rest of this week, but I'll see you on Saturday. Be ready by eight o'clock.'

When he rang off, she stood for a moment, happy once more, planning to buy a dress fit for the occasion. Her father paid her a salary for working in the shop and she had saved most of it... She went to find her mother to tell her.

There was only a handful of dress shops in the town, and since her father didn't have a car, and the bus service, now that the season was over, had shrunk to market day and Saturday, Totnes and Plymouth were out of the question. Daisy visited each of the boutiques in the high street and to her relief found a dress—red, and not, she considered, quite her style, but red was what Desmond wanted...

She took it home and tried it on again—and wished she hadn't bought it; it was far too short, and hardly decent—not her kind of a dress at all. When she showed it to her mother she could see that that lady thought the same. But Mrs Gillard loved her daughter, and wanted her to be happy. She observed that the dress was just right for an evening out and prayed silently that Desmond, whom she didn't like, would be sent by his firm, whoever they were, to the other end of the country.

Saturday came, and Daisy, in a glow of excitement, dressed for the evening, did her face carefully and pinned her hair into a topknot more suitable for a sober schoolteacher's outfit than the red dress, then went downstairs to wait for Desmond.

He kept her waiting for ten minutes, for which he offered no apology, and her mother and father, greeting him civilly, wished that Daisy could have fallen in love with any man but he. He made a great business of studying the dress. 'Quite OK,' he told her airily, and then frowned. 'Of course your hair is all wrong, but it's too late to do anything to it now...'

There were a great many people at the hotel, milling around waiting to go into dinner, and several of them hailed Desmond as they joined them. When Desmond introduced her, they nodded casually, then ignored her. Not that she minded that. She stood quietly listening to Desmond. He was a clever talker, knowing how to keep his listeners interested, and she could see that he was charming them.

She took the glass of wine she was offered and they made their way through the crowded foyer, stopping from time to time to greet someone Desmond knew, sometimes so briefly that he didn't bother to introduce her. They sat with a party of eight in the restaurant, and presently Desmond, already dominating the talk at the table, made no attempt to include her in it. The man on her other side was young, with a loud voice, and he asked her who she was.

'Came with Des? Not his usual type, are you? Cunning rascal wants to catch the eye of the guest of honour—he's an influential old fellow, very strait-laced—thinks all young men should marry and settle down with a little woman and a horde of children. The plainer the better.' He laughed. 'You're just the ticket, if I may say so.'

Daisy gave him a long, cold stare, suppressed a desire to slap his face, and instead chose a morsel of whatever it was on her plate and popped it in her mouth. If it hadn't been for Desmond's presence beside her she would have got up and walked out but he had impressed upon her the importance of the evening; his chance to meet the right people...

She sat through dinner, ignoring the awful man on her left and wishing that Desmond would speak to her. Only he was deep in conversation with the elegant woman on his right, and, from time to time, joining in talk with other people at the table. Perhaps it would be better once they started the dancing...

Only it wasn't. True, he danced the first dance with her, whirling her around in a flashy fashion, but then he told her, 'I must talk to a few people once this dance is over. Shan't be long; you'll get plenty of partners—you dance quite well. Only do, for heaven's sake, look as though you're enjoying yourself. I know it's a bit above you, Daisy, but don't let it intimidate you.'

He waved to someone across the ballroom. 'I must go and have a word, I'll be back,' he assured her, leaving her pressed up against a wall between a large statue holding a lamp and a pedestal holding an elaborate flower arrangement. She felt hemmed in and presently, when Desmond didn't come back, lonely.

One side of the ballroom was open onto the corridor leading to the restaurant, and two men strolling along it paused to look at the dancers, talking quietly together. Presently they shook hands and the older man went on his way. His companion stayed where he was, in no hurry to leave, his attention caught by Daisy's red dress. He studied her at some length. She didn't look as though she belonged, and that dress was all wrong…

He strolled round the edge of the ballroom towards her, vaguely wishing to help her in some way. Close to her now, he could see that she wasn't pretty, and looked prim, definitely out of place on the noisy dance floor. He stopped beside her and said in a friendly voice, 'Are you like me? a stranger here?'

Daisy looked up at him, wondering why she hadn't noticed him before, for he was a man who could hardly go unnoticed. Tall, very tall, and heavily built, with handsome features and grey hair cut short. He had a commanding nose and a rather thin mouth, but he was smiling at her in a reassuring way.

She said politely, 'Well, yes, I am, but I came with someone—he has friends here. I don't know anyone…'

Jules der Huizma was adept at putting people at their ease. He began a gentle rambling conversation about nothing in particular and watched her relax. Quite a pleasant girl, he reflected. A shame about the dress…

He stayed with her until presently he saw a man making his way towards them. When Desmond reached them, Mr der Huizma nodded in a friendly fashion and wandered away.

'Who was that?' demanded Desmond.

'I've no idea—another guest?' Daisy added with unexpected tartness, 'It was pleasant to have someone to talk with.'

Desmond said too quickly, 'Darling, I'm sorry,' and he gave her a smile to quicken her heartbeat. 'I'll make it up to you. I've been asked to go on to a nightclub in Plymouth—quite a jolly crowd. You can come too, of course. Another one won't matter.'

'Plymouth? But, Desmond, it's almost midnight. You said you would take me home then. Of course I can't go. In any case I wasn't invited, was I?'

'Well, no, but who's to mind? Another girl won't matter, and good Lord, Daisy, let yourself go for once—' He broke off as a girl joined them. A pretty girl, slim and dressed in the height of fashion, teetering on four-inch heels, swinging a sequinned bag, tossing fashionably tousled hair.

'Des—there you are. We're waiting.'

She glanced at Daisy and he said quickly, 'This is Daisy; she came with me.' He spoke sharply, 'Daisy, this is Tessa.'

'Oh, well, I suppose one more won't matter. There'll be room for her in one of the cars.' Tessa smiled vaguely.

'It's kind of you to ask me,' said Daisy, 'but I said I would be home by midnight.'

Tessa's eyes opened wide and she laughed. 'A proper little Cinderella, though that frock's all wrong—you're too mousy to wear red.' She turned to Desmond. 'Take Cinderella home, Des. I'll wait here for you.'

She turned on her ridiculous heels and was lost among the dancers.

Daisy waited for Desmond to say something, to tell her that he wouldn't go with Tessa.

'OK, I'll take you home, but for heaven's sake be quick getting your coat. I'll be at the entrance.' He spoke in an angry voice. 'You're doing your best to ruin my evening.'

Daisy said woodenly, 'And what about my evening?'

But he had turned away, and she wasn't sure if he had heard.

It took her a minute or two to find her coat under a pile of others in the alcove close to the entrance. She was putting it on when she became aware of voices from the other side of the screen.

'Sorry you had to hang around for me, Jules. Shall we go along to the bar? There is still a great deal to talk about and I'm glad of the chance to see you after all this time. Wish it had been quieter here, though. Not much of an evening for you. I hope you found someone interesting to talk to.'

'I found someone.' Daisy recognised the voice of the man who had been so pleasant. 'A plain little creature in a regrettable red dress. A fish out of water…'

They moved away, and Daisy, not allowing herself to think, went to the entrance, where Desmond was waiting. He drove her home in silence, and only as she was getting out of the car did he speak. He said, unforgivably, 'You look silly in that dress.'

Funnily enough, that didn't hurt her half as much as the strange man's opinion had done.

The house was quiet, with no light showing. She went in through the side door, along the passage to her father's office and up the stairs to her room—small, but charmingly furnished with pieces she had chosen from the shop, none of it matching but all of it harmonising nicely. There was a patchwork quilt on the narrow bed, and plain white curtains at the small window, and a small bookshelf bulging with books.

She undressed quickly and then parcelled up the red dress to hand over to the charity shop in the high street. She would have liked to have taken a pair of scissors and cut it into shreds, but that would have been a stupid thing to do; somewhere there must be a girl who would look just right in it. Daisy got into bed as the church clock chimed one and lay wide awake, going over the wreck of her evening. She still loved Desmond; she was sure of that. People in love quarrelled, even in her euphoric state she was aware of that, and of course he had been disappointed—she hadn't come up to his expectations and he had said a great many things she was sure he would regret.

Daisy, such a sensible, matter-of-fact girl, was quite blinded by her infatuation, and ready to make any excuses for Desmond. She closed her eyes, determined to sleep. In the morning everything would be just as it had been again.

Only it wasn't. She wasn't sure what she'd expected—a phone call? A quick visit? He seemed to have plenty time on his hands.

She busied herself arranging a small display of Coalport china, reflecting that she knew almost nothing about his work or how he spent his days. When he took her out in the evenings he would answer her queries as to his day with some light-hearted remark which actually told her nothing. But, despite the disappointment and humiliation of the previous evening, she was quite prepared to listen to his apologies—might even laugh about the disastrous evening with him.

Even while she consoled herself with these thoughts, good sense was telling her that she was behaving like a naive teenager, although she was reluctant to admit it. Desmond represented romance in her quiet life.

He didn't phone, he didn't come to see her, and it was several days later that she saw him on the other side of the high street. He must have seen her, for the street was almost empty, but he walked on, to all intents and purpose a complete stranger.

Daisy went back to the shop and spent the rest of the day packing up a set of antique wine glasses which an old customer had bought. It was a slow, careful job, and it gave her ample time to think. One thing was clear to her; Desmond didn't love her—never had, she admitted sadly. True, he had called her darling, and kissed her and told her that she was his dream girl, but he hadn't meant a word of it. She had been happy to believe him; romance, for her, had been rather lacking, and he had seemed like the answer to her romantic dreams. But the romance had been only on her side.

She wedged the last glass into place in its nest of tissue paper and put the lid on the box. And at the same time she told herself, I've put a lid on Desmond too, and I'll never be romantic again—once bitten…!

All the same, the next weeks were hard going. It had been easy to get into the habit of seeing Desmond several times a week. She tried to fill the gaps by going to films, or having coffee with friends, but that wasn't entirely successful for they all had boyfriends or were engaged, and it was difficult to maintain a carefree indifference as to her own future in the face of their friendly probings. She got thinner, and spent more time than she needed to in the shop, so that her mother coaxed her to go out more.

'There's not much doing in the shop at this time of year,' she observed. 'Why not have a good walk in the afternoons, love? It will soon be too cold and dark, and there'll be all the extra custom with Christmas.'

So Daisy went out walking. Mostly the same walk, down to the sea, to tramp along the sand, well wrapped up against the early November wind and rain. She met a few other hardy souls; people she knew by sight, walking their dogs. They shouted cheerful greetings as they passed and she shouted back, her voice carried away on the wind.

It was during the last week of November that Daisy met once more the man who had likened her to a fish out of water. Jules der Huizma was spending a few days with his friend again, at his house some miles out of the town, enjoying the quiet country life after the hurry and stress of London. He loved the sea; it reminded him of his own country.

He saw her some way ahead of him and recognised her at once. She was walking into the teeth of a chilly wind bearing cold drizzle with it, and he lengthened his stride, whistling to his friend's dog so that it ran on ahead of him. He had no wish to take her by surprise, and Trigger's cheerful barks would slow her down or cause her to turn round.

They did both. She stopped to pat his elderly head and looked over her shoulder; she greeted him politely in a cool voice, his words at the hotel still very clear in her head. And then forgot to be cool when he said, 'How delightful to meet someone who likes walking in the rain and the wind.'

He smiled at her as he spoke, and she forgave him then for calling her a fish out of water—a plain fish too. After all, in all fairness she had been both. Indeed, when it came to being plain she would always be that.

They walked on side by side, not talking too much for the wind was too fierce, and presently, by mutual consent, they turned back towards the town, climbed the steps and walked up the main street. At the corner of the lane, Daisy paused. 'I live down here with my mother and father. Father has an antiques shop and I work there.'

Mr der Huizma saw that he was being dismissed politely. 'Then I hope that at some time I shall have the opportunity to browse there. I'm interested in old silver...'

'So is Father. He's quite well known for being an expert.'

She put out a wet gloved hand. 'I enjoyed the walk.' She studied his quiet face. 'I don't know your name...'

'Jules der Huizma.'

'Not English? I'm Daisy Gillard.'

He took her small damp paw in a firm grip. 'I too enjoyed the walk,' he told her gently. 'Perhaps we shall meet again some time.'

'Yes, well—perhaps.' She added, 'Goodbye,' and walked down the lane, not looking back. A pity, she thought, that I couldn't think of something clever to say, so that he would want to see me again. She remembered Desmond then, and told herself not to be so stupid; he wasn't in the least bit like Desmond, but who was it that wrote 'Men were deceivers ever'? Probably they were all alike.

She took care for the next few days to walk the other way—which was pointless since Mr der Huizma had gone back to London.

A week or so later, with the shops displaying

Christmas goods and a lighted Christmas tree at the top of the high street opposite the church, she met him again. Only this time it was at the shop. Daisy was waiting patiently by the vicar, while he tried to decide which of two Edwardian brooches his wife would like. She left him with a murmured suggestion that he might like to take his time and went through the shop to where Mr der Huizma was stooping over a glass-topped display table housing a collection of silver charms.

He greeted her pleasantly. 'I'm looking for something for a teenage god-daughter. These are delightful—on a silver bracelet, perhaps?'

She opened a drawer in the large bow-fronted tallboy and took out a tray.

'These are all Victorian. Is she a little girl or an older teenager?'

'Fifteen or so.' He smiled down at her. 'And very fashion-conscious.'

Daisy held up a dainty trifle of silver links. 'If you should wish to buy it, and the charms, Father will fasten them on for you.' She picked up another bracelet. 'Or this? Please just look around. You don't need to buy anything—a lot of people just come to browse.'

She gave him a small smile and went back to the vicar, who was still unable to make up his mind.

Presently her father came into the shop, and when

at last the vicar had made his decision, and she'd wrapped the brooch in a pretty box, Mr der Huizma had gone.

'Did he buy anything?' asked Daisy. 'Mr der Huizma? Remember I told you I met him one day out walking?'

'Indeed he did. A very knowledgeable man too. He's coming back before Christmas—had his eye on those rat-tailed spoons…'

And two days later Desmond came into the shop. He wasn't alone. The girl Daisy had met at the hotel was with him, wrapped in a scarlet leather coat and wearing a soft angora cap on her expertly disarranged locks. Daisy, eyeing her, felt like a mouse in her colourless dress; a garment approved of by her father, who considered that a brighter one would detract from the treasures in his shop.

She would have liked to have turned away, gone out of the shop, but that would have been cowardly. She answered Desmond's careless, 'Hullo, Daisy,' with composure, even if her colour was heightened, and listened politely while he explained at some length that they were just having a look round. 'We might pick up some trifle which will do for Christmas…'

'Silver? Gold?' asked Daisy. 'Or there are some pretty little china ornaments if you don't want to spend too much.'

Which wasn't a polite thing to say, but her tongue had said it before she could curb it. It gave her some satisfaction to see Desmond's annoyance, even though at the same time she had to admit to a sudden wish that he would look at her—really look—and realise that he was in love with *her* and not with the girl in the red coat. It was a satisfying thought, but nonsense, of course, and, when she thought about it, it struck her that perhaps she hadn't loved him after all. All the same, he had left a hole in her quiet life. And her pride had been hurt…

They stayed for some time and left without buying anything, Desmond pointing out in a rather too loud voice that they were more likely to find something worth buying if they went to Plymouth. A remark which finally did away with Daisy's last vestige of feeling towards him…

During her solitary afternoon walks, shorter now that the Christmas rush had started, she decided that she would never allow herself to get fond of a man again. Not that there was much chance of that, she reflected. She was aware that she was lacking in good looks, that she would never be slender like the models in the glossy magazines, that she lacked the conversation likely to charm a man.

She had friends whom she had known for most of her life; most of them were married now, or working in some high-powered job. But for Daisy, once she had managed to get a couple of A levels, the future had been an obvious one. She had grown up amongst antiques, she loved them, and she had her father's talent for finding them. Once she'd realised that she'd studied books about them, had gone to auctions and poked around dingy little back-street second hand shops, occasionally finding a genuine piece. And her father and mother, while making no effort to coerce her, had been well content that she should stay home, working in the shop and from time to time visiting some grand country house whose owners were compelled to sell its contents.

They had discussed the idea of her going to a university and getting a degree, but that would have meant her father getting an assistant, and although they lived comfortably enough his income depended very much on circumstances.

So Daisy had arranged her future in what she considered to be a sensible manner.

She thought no more about Desmond. But she did think about Mr der Huizma—thoughts about him creeping into her head at odd moments. He was someone she would have liked to know better; his calm, friendly manner had been very soothing to her hurt feelings, and he seemed to accept her for what she was—a very ordinary girl. His matter-of-fact manner towards her was somehow reassuring.

But there wasn't much time to daydream now; the

shop was well known, Mr Gillard was known to be an honest man, and very knowledgeable, and old customers came back year after year, seeking some trifle to give as a present. Some returned to buy an antique piece they had had their eye on for months, having decided that they might indulge their taste now, since it was Christmas.

Daisy, arranging a small display of antique toys on a cold, dark December morning, wished that she was a child again so that she might play with the Victorian dolls' house she was furnishing with all the miniature pieces which went with it. It had been a lucky find in a down-at-heel shop in Plymouth—dirty and in need of careful repair. Something she had lovingly undertaken. Now it stood in a place of honour on a small side-table, completely furnished and flanked by a cased model of a nineteenth century butcher's shop and a toy grocery shop from pre-war Germany.

All very expensive, but someone might buy them. She would have liked the dolls' house for herself; whoever bought that would need to have a very deep pocket…

Apparently Mr der Huizma had just that, for he came that very day and, after spending a considerable time examining spoons with her father, wandered over to where she was putting the finishing touches to a tinplate carousel.

He bent to look at the dolls' house. She wished him good morning, then said in her quiet voice, 'Charming, isn't it? A little girl's dream…'

'Yes? You consider that to be so?'

'Oh, yes. Only she would have to be a careful little girl, who liked dolls.'

'Then I'll buy it, for I know exactly the little girl you think should own it.'

'You do? It's a lot of money…'

'But she is a dear child who deserves only the best.'

Daisy would have liked to have known more, but something in his voice stopped her from asking. She said merely, 'Shall I pack it up for you? I'll do it very carefully. It will take some time if you want it sent. If you do, I'll get it properly boxed.'

'No, no. I'll take it with me in the car. Can you have it ready in a few days if I call back for it?'

'Yes.'

'I shall be taking it out of the country.'

Going home for Christmas, thought Daisy, and said, 'I'll be extra careful, and I'll give you an invoice just in case Customs should want to know about it.'

He smiled at her. 'How very efficient you are, and how glad I am that I have found the house; presents for small children are always a problem.'

'Do you have several children?'

His smile widened. 'We are a large family,' he told her, and with that she had to be satisfied.

CHAPTER TWO

PACKING up the dolls' house, wrapping each tiny piece of furniture carefully in tissue paper, writing an inventory of its contents, took Daisy an entire day, and gave her ample time to reflect upon Mr der Huizma. Who exactly was he? she wondered. A man of some wealth to buy such a costly gift for a child, and a man of leisure, presumably, for he had never mentioned work of any kind. And did he live in England, or merely visit England from time to time? And if so where did he live?

Mr der Huizma, unaware of Daisy's interest in him and, truth to tell, uncaring of it, was strolling down the centre of the children's ward of a London teaching hospital. He had a toddler tucked under one arm—a small, damp grizzling boy, who had been sobbing so loudly that the only thing to do was to pick him up and comfort him as Mr der Huizma did his round. Sister was beside him, middle-aged, prematurely grey-haired and as thin as a rail. None of these things were noticed, though, for she had the disposition of an angel and very beautiful dark blue eyes.

She said now, 'He'll ruin that suit of yours, sir,'

and then, when he smiled down at her, asked, 'What do you intend to do about him? He's made no progress at all.'

Mr der Huizma paused in his stride and was instantly surrounded by a posse of lesser medical lights and an earnest-faced nurse holding the case-sheets.

He hoisted the little boy higher onto his shoulder. 'Only one thing for it,' He glanced at his registrar. 'Tomorrow morning? Will you see Theatre Sister as early as possible? And let his parents know, will you? I'll talk to them this evening if they'd like to visit…'

He continued his round, unhurried, sitting on cot-sides to talk to the occupants, examining children in a leisurely fashion, giving instructions in a quiet voice. Presently he went to Sister's office and drank his coffee with her and his registrar and the two housemen. The talk was of Christmas, and plans for the ward. A tree, of course, and stockings hung on the bed and filled with suitable toys, paper chains, and mothers and fathers coming to a splendid tea.

Mr der Huizma listened to the small talk, saying little himself. He would be here on the ward on Christmas morning, after flying over from Holland in his plane very early, and would return home during the afternoon. He had done that ever since he'd taken up his appointment as senior paediatrician at the hospital, doing it without fuss, and presenting himself at the hospital in Amsterdam on the following day to join in the festivities on the children's ward there—and somehow he managed to spend time with his family too...

A few days before Christmas he called at the shop to collect the dolls' house. Daisy, absorbed in cleaning a very dirty emerald necklace—a find in someone's attic and sold to her father by its delighted owner—glanced round as he came into the shop, put down the necklace and waved a hand at the dolls' house shrouded in its wrappings.

'It's all ready. Do take care not to jog it about too much. Everything is packed tightly, but it would be awful if anything broke.'

He wished her good evening gravely, and added, 'I'll be careful. And we will unpack it and check everything before Mies sees it.'

'Mies—what a pretty name. I'm sure she will love it. How old is she?'

He didn't answer at once, and she wished she hadn't asked. 'She is five years old,' he said presently.

She wanted to ask if he had any more children, but sensed that he wasn't a man who would welcome such questions. Instead she said, 'I'll get Father to give you a hand—have you a car outside?'

When he nodded, she asked, 'Are you going back

to Holland today?' She sighed without knowing it. 'Your family will be glad to see you...'

He said gravely, 'I hope so. Christmas is a time for families, is it not?' He studied her quiet face. 'And you? Do you also attend a family gathering?'

'Me? Oh, no. I mean there isn't a family—just Mother and Father and me.' She added quickly, 'But we have a lovely Christmas.'

Mr der Huizma, thinking of his own family gathered at his home, wondered if that were true. She didn't seem a girl to hanker after bright lights, but surely Christmas spent over the shop with only her parents for company would be dull. He dismissed a vague feeling of concern for her as her father came into the shop; theirs had been a chance meeting and they were unlikely to see each other again.

He and Mr Gillard carried the dolls' house out to his car, and before he drove away he came back into the shop to thank her for her work with it, wish her a happy Christmas and bid her goodbye.

There was an air of finality about his words; Daisy knew with regret that she would not see him again.

She thought about him a good deal during Christmas. The shop was busy until the last minute of Christmas Eve, and Christmas Day was filled to the brim, with the morning ritual of opening their presents, going to church and sitting down to the traditional dinner in the late afternoon. On Boxing

Day she had visited friends in the town and joined a party of them in the evening—all the same, she found time to wonder about him…

And of course on the following day the shop was open again. It was surprising what a number of ungrateful recipients of trinkets and sets of sherry glasses and china ornaments were anxious to turn them into cash. And then there was a lull. Money was scarce after Christmas, and customers were few and far between, which gave Daisy time to clean and polish and repair with her small capable hands while her father was away for a few days at an auction being held on one of the small estates in the north of the country.

He came back well satisfied; not only had he made successful bids for a fine set of silver Georgian tea caddies and a pair of George the Second sauce boats, but he had also acquired a Dutch painted and gilt leather screen, eighteenth-century and in an excellent condition—although the chinoiserie figures were almost obscured by years of ingrained dirt and dust. It had been found in one of the attics and had attracted little attention. He had paid rather more than he could afford for it, and there was always the chance that it would stay in the shop, unsold and representing a considerable loss to him. But on the other hand he might sell it advantageously…

It fell to Daisy's lot to clean and restore it to a

pristine state, something which took days of patient work. It was a slow business, and she had ample opportunity to think. It was surprising how often her thoughts dwelt on Mr der Huizma, which, considering she wasn't going to see him again, seemed a great waste of time.

It was towards the end of January, with the screen finished and business getting brisker, when two elderly men came into the shop. They greeted her with courtesy, and a request that they might look around the shop, and wandered to and fro at some length, murmuring to each other, stooping down to admire some trifle which had caught their eye. Daisy, whose ears were sharp, decided that they were murmuring in a foreign language. But they spoke English well enough when her father came into the shop, passing the time of day with him as they continued their leisurely progress.

They stopped abruptly when they saw the screen, right at the back of the shop. For two calm, elderly gentlemen they exhibited a sudden interest tinged with excitement. There was no need for her father to describe it to them; it seemed that they knew as much about it as he did, possibly more. They examined it at length and with great care, asked its price, and without further argument took out a chequebook.

'I must explain,' said one gentleman, and Daisy

edged nearer so as not to miss a word. 'This screen—you tell me that you bought it at an auction at the Kings Poulton estate? I must tell you that an ancestress of ours married a member of the family in the eighteenth century and brought this screen with her as part of her dowry. It was made especially for her. You will have seen the initials at the edge of the border—her initials. When we were last in England we enquired about it but were told that it had been destroyed in the fire they had some years ago. You can imagine our delight in discovering that it is safe—and in such splendid condition.'

'You must thank my daughter for that,' said Mr Gillard. 'It was in a shocking state.'

The three of them turned and looked at her. She smiled nicely at them, for the two elderly gentlemen were friendly, and she was intrigued by the screen's history and the chance discovery they had made of it. 'It is very beautiful,' she said. 'I don't know where you live, but you'll need to be very careful with it; it's fragile…'

'It must return, of course, to our home in Holland—near Amsterdam. And we can assure you, young lady, that it will be transported with great care.'

'In a van, properly packed,' said Daisy.

The elder of the two gentlemen, the one with the forbidding nose and flowing moustache, said meekly,

'Most certainly, and with a reliable courier.' He paused, and then exchanged a look with his companion.

'Perhaps you would undertake the task of bringing the screen to Holland, young lady? Since you have restored it you will know best how it should be handled, and possibly you will remain for a brief period to ensure that no harm has come to it on the journey.'

'Me?' Daisy sounded doubtful. 'Well, of course I'd love to do that, but I'm not an expert, or qualified or anything like that.'

'But you would do this if we ask you?'

She glanced at her father.

'A good idea, Daisy, and you are perfectly capable of doing it. You'll need a day for travelling, and another day for the return journey, and a day or two to check that everything is as it should be.'

'Very well, I'll be glad to do that. I'll need a couple of days in which to pack the screen…'

The moustached gentleman offered a hand. 'Thank you. If we may return in the morning and discuss the details? I am Heer van der Breek.'

Daisy took the hand. 'Daisy Gillard. I'm glad you found your screen.'

His companion shook hands too, and then they bade her father goodbye.

When they had gone, Daisy said, 'You're sure I can do it? I can't speak Dutch, Father.'

'No problem, and of course you can do it, a sensible girl like you, my dear. Besides, while you're there you can go to Heer Friske's shop in Amsterdam—remember he wrote and told me that he had a Georgian wine cooler I might be interested in? Colonel Gibbs has been wanting one, and if you think it's a genuine piece you might buy it and bring it back with you.'

'Where will I stay?' asked the practical Daisy.

'Oh, there must be plenty of small hotels—he will probably know of one.'

It was surprising how quickly matters were arranged. In rather less than a week Daisy found herself sitting beside the driver of the small van housing the screen on her way to Holland. She had money, her passport, and directions in her handbag, a travelling bag stuffed with everything necessary for a few days' stay in that country, and all the documents necessary for a trouble-free journey. She was to stay at Meneer van der Breek's house and oversee the unpacking of the screen and its installation, and from there she was to go to Amsterdam and present herself at Mijnheer Friske's shop. A small hotel close by had been found for her and she was to stay as long as it was necessary. Two or three days should be sufficient, her father had told her.

Excited under her calm exterior, Daisy settled

back to enjoy her trip. Her companion was of a friendly disposition, pleased to have company, and before long she was listening with a sympathetic ear to his disappointment at missing his eldest daughter's birthday. 'Though I'll buy her something smashing in Amsterdam,' he assured her. 'This kind of job is too well paid to refuse.'

They crossed on the overnight ferry, and since Mijnheer van der Breek had made all the arrangements for their journey it went without a hitch and in comfort.

It was raining when they disembarked in the early morning, and Daisy, looking around her, reflected that this flat and damp landscape wasn't at all what she had expected. But presently there was a watery winter sun, and the built-up areas were left behind. They stopped for coffee, and then drove on.

'Loenen aan de Vecht,' said the driver. 'The other side of Amsterdam on the way to Utrecht. Not far now—we turn off the motorway soon.'

He bypassed Amsterdam and emerged into quiet countryside, and presently onto a country road running beside a river. 'The Vecht,' said Daisy, poring over the map.

It was a delightful road, tree-lined, with here and there a pleasant house tucked away. On the opposite bank there were more houses—rather grand gentlemen's residences, with sweeping lawns bordering the water and surrounded by trees and shrubs.

Before long they came to a bridge and crossed it.

'Is it here?' asked Daisy. 'One of these houses? They're rather splendid…'

They turned in through wrought-iron gates and drew up before an imposing doorway reached by stone steps. There were rows of orderly windows with heavy shutters and gabled roofs above the house's solid face, and an enormous bell-pull beside the door. Daisy got out and looked around her with knowledgeable eyes. Seventeenth-century, she guessed, and probably older than that round the back.

The driver had got out too and rung the bell; they could hear its sonorous clanging somewhere in the depths of the house. Presently the door was opened by a stout man, and Daisy handed over the letter Mijnheer van der Breek had given her in England.

Invited to step inside, she did so, prudently asking the driver to stay with the van, and was led down a long, gloomy hall to big double doors at its end. The stout man flung them open and crossed the large and equally gloomy apartment to where Mijnheer van der Breek sat. He handed him the letter and waved Daisy forward.

Mijnheer van der Breek got up, shook hands with her and asked, 'You have the screen? Splendid. It is unfortunate that my brother is indisposed, otherwise he would have shared my pleasure at your arrival.'

'It's outside in the van,' said Daisy. 'If you would tell me where you want it put the driver and I will see to it.'

'No, no, young lady. Cor shall help the man. Although you must supervise its removal, of course. We have decided that we want it in the salon. When it has been brought there I will come personally and say where it is to go.'

Daisy would have liked five minutes' leisure, preferably with a pot of tea, but it seemed that she wasn't to get it. She went back to the van, this time with Cor, and watched while the men took the screen from the van and carried it carefully into the house. More double doors on one side of the hall had been opened, and she followed them into the room beyond. It was large and lofty, with tall narrow windows heavily swathed in crimson velvet curtains. The furniture was antique, but not of a period which Daisy cared for—dark and heavy and vaguely Teutonic. But, she had to admit, a good background for the screen.

Time was taken in getting the screen just so, and she finally heard Mijnheer van der Breek's satisfied approval. What was more, he told her that she might postpone unwrapping it and examining it until after they had had luncheon. It was only after he had seen his treasure safely disposed that he sent for his housekeeper to show Daisy her room.

Daisy bade the driver goodbye, reminded him to drive carefully and to let her father know that they had arrived safely, and followed the imposing bulk of the housekeeper up the elaborately carved staircase.

She was led away from the gallery above and down a small passage, down a pair of steps, along another passage, and then finally into a room at the corner of the house with windows in two walls, a lofty ceiling and a canopied bed. The floor was polished wood, with thick rugs here and there. A small table with two chairs drawn up to it was in one corner of the room, and there was a pier table with a marble top holding a Dutch marquetry toilet mirror flanked by a pair of ugly but valuable Imari vases. The room was indeed a treasure house of antiques, although none to her liking. But the adjoining bathroom won her instant approval. She tidied her hair, did her face and found her way downstairs, hopeful of lunch.

It was eaten in yet another room, somewhat smaller than the others, but splendidly furnished, the table laid with damask cloth and a good deal of very beautiful silver and china. A pity that the meal didn't live up to its opulent surroundings.

'A light lunch at midday,' explained Mijnheer van

der Breek, and indeed it was. A spoonful or two of clear soup, a dish of cold meats, another of cheeses, and a basket of rolls, partaken of so sparingly by her host that she felt unable to satisfy her appetite. But the coffee was delicious.

Probably dinner would be a more substantial meal, hoped Daisy, rising from the table with her host and, since he expected it of her, going to examine the screen.

She spent the afternoon carefully checking every inch of the screen; removing every speck of dust, making sure that the light wasn't too strong for it, making sure that the gilt wasn't damaged. She hardly noticed the time passing, and she stopped thankfully when the housekeeper brought her a small tray of tea. She worked on then, until she was warned that dinner would be at seven o'clock. She went to her room and changed into a plain brown jersey dress which didn't do nothing to improve her appearance but which didn't crease when packed…

Both elderly gentlemen were at dinner, so that she was kept busy answering their questions during the meal—a substantial one, she was glad to find; pork cutlets with cooked beetroot, braised chicory and large floury potatoes smothered in butter. Pudding was a kind of blancmange with a fruit sauce. Good solid fare. Either the gentlemen didn't have a good cook or they had no fancy for more elaborate cooking. But once again the coffee was delicious. Over it they discussed her departure.

'Perhaps tomorrow afternoon?' suggested Mijnheer van der Breek, and glanced at his brother, who nodded. 'You will be driven to Amsterdam,' she was told. 'We understand that you have an errand there for your father. We are most grateful for your help in bringing the screen to us, but I am sure that you would wish to fulfil your commission and return home as soon as possible.'

Daisy smiled politely and reflected that, much as she loved her home, it was delightful to be on her own in a strange country. She would see as much of Amsterdam as possible while she was there. She would phone her father as soon as she could and ask him if she might stay another day there—there were museums she dearly wanted to see…

She was driven to Amsterdam the next day by the stout man in an elderly and beautifully maintained Daimler. The hotel her father had chosen for her was small and welcoming, down a small side-street criss-crossed by canals. The proprietor spoke English, and led her up a steep staircase to a small room overlooking the street. He reminded her that the evening meal was at six o'clock, then went back to his cubby-hole by the entrance.

It was a gloomy afternoon, already turned to dusk. Too late to visit Heer Friske's shop, so Daisy contented herself with tidying her person, unpacking her few clothes and then sitting down in the overstuffed chair by the window to study a map of the city. Complicated, she decided, as she found the small square where Heer Friske had his shop. But she had all day before her on the morrow and, since her father had had no objection to her staying for a second day, she would have a whole further day sightseeing before going back on the night ferry.

She went downstairs presently, to the small dining room in the basement, and found a dozen other people there, all of them Dutch. They greeted her kindly and, being a friendly girl by nature, she enjoyed her meal. Soup, pork chops with ample potatoes and vegetables, and a custard for pudding. Simple, compared with the fare at Mijnheer van der Breek's house, but much more sustaining…

She slept well, ate her breakfast of rolls and cheese and cold meat, drank several cups of coffee and, thus fortified, started off for Heer Friske's shop. The hotel didn't provide lunch, and in any case she didn't intend to return before the late afternoon. As she started to pick her way through the various streets she saw plenty of small coffee shops where she would be able to get a midday snack.

She missed her way several times, but, being a sensible girl, she didn't get flustered. All the same, she was glad when she reached the shop. It was small and old and the window was crammed with small antiques. She spent a minute or two studying them before she entered the shop. It was dark inside, lighted by rather feeble wall-lights, and extended back into even deeper gloom. The whole place was crowded with antiques. Daisy made her way carefully towards the old man sitting at a desk in the middle of it all.

She said, 'Good morning,' and offered a hand, guessing quite rightly that he wasn't the kind of man who would waste time on unnecessary chat, for he barely glanced at her before resuming the polishing of a rather fine silver coffee pot.

'Daisy Gillard,' said Daisy clearly. 'You told my father that you had a Georgian wine cooler. May I see it, please?'

Heer Friske found his voice and spoke in strongly accented English. 'You are here to buy it? You are capable?'

'My father thinks so.'

He got up slowly and led her further into the shop, where the wine cooler stood on top of a solid table. He didn't say anything, but stood back while she examined it. It was a splendid specimen, in good condition and genuine. 'How much?' asked Daisy.

His price was too high, but she had expected that. It took half an hour's bargaining over several cups of coffee before they reached an amount which pleased them both. Daisy made out a Eurocheque, said that she would return on the following day to make arrangements to convey the unwieldy cooler to the station, and took her leave, pleased with herself and happy to have the rest of the day in which to do exactly what she liked.

By the time she got back to the hotel in the late afternoon she was tired but content; she had crammed the Rijksmuseum, two churches, Anne Frank's house and a canal trip into her time, stopping only for a brief while to consume a *kaas broodje* and a cup of coffee.

At dinner she told her companions where she had been and they nodded approval, pointing out that the evening was when she should take the opportunity of walking to the Leidesplein to get a glimpse of the brightly lighted square with its cafés and hotels and cheerful crowds.

Daisy, a cock-a-hoop over her successful day, decided that she would do just that. It was no distance, and although it was a chilly night, with a sparkling frost, there was a moon and plenty of people around. She found her way to the Leidesplein easily enough, had a cup of coffee at a street stall while she watched the evening crowds, and then started back to the hotel.

However, somehow she mistook her way, and, turning round to check where she had come from, took unguarded steps backwards and fell into a canal.

She came to the surface of the icy water and her first thought was thankfulness that she hadn't had anything valuable about her person; the second was a flash of panic. The water wasn't just cold, it smelled awful—and tasted worse. There were probably rats… She opened her mouth and bawled for help and swam, very hampered by her clothes, to the canal bank. Slippery stones, too steep for her to scramble up. She bawled again, and, miracle of miracles, a firm hand caught her shoulder while a second grabbed her other arm, almost wrenching it from its socket. She was heaved onto the street with no more ado.

'Not hurt?' asked her rescuer.

'Ugh,' said Daisy, and was thankfully sick, half kneeling on the cobbles.

'Only very wet and—er, strong-smelling,' added a voice she knew.

He bent and set her on her feet. 'Come with me and we'll get you cleaned up.'

'Mr der Huizma,' said Daisy. 'Oh, it would be you, wouldn't it?' she added wildly. It was nice to have been rescued, but why couldn't it have been by a stranger? Why did it have to be someone who, if he'd remembered her at all, would have thought of her as a quiet, well-mannered girl with a knowledge of antiques and a liking for walks by the sea. Now it would be as a silly, careless fool.

'Indeed it is I.' He had her by the arm. 'Across this bridge is the hospital where I work. They will soon have you clean and dry again. You didn't lose anything in the canal?'

'No. I didn't have more than a few *gulden* with me. I only turned round to see where I was...'

'Of course,' agreed Mr der Huizma gravely, 'a perfectly natural thing to do. This way.'

The hospital was indeed close by. He led her, squelching and dripping, into the casualty entrance and handed her over to a large bony woman who clucked sympathetically and led Daisy away before she had time to utter a word of thanks to Mr der Huizma. Her clothes were taken from her, she was put under a hot shower, her hair was washed and she was given injections. The sister, who spoke good English, smiled at her. 'Rats,' she said, plunging in the needle. 'A precaution.'

She was given hot coffee, wrapped in a hospital gown several sizes too large and a thick blanket, and sat on a chair in one of the cubicles. She felt quite restored in her person, but her mind was in a fine jumble. She had no clothes; her own had been taken away, but even if they were washed they would never be dry enough, and how was she to get back to the hotel? No one had asked her that yet. She rubbed her long mousy hair dry and began to worry.

The cubicle curtains were parted and Sister appeared; looming beside her was Mr der Huizma. Daisy stared up at them from the depths of her blanket.

'My clothes? If I could have…?'

Sister interrupted her in a kind, forceful voice. 'Mr der Huizma will take you back to your hotel and explain what has happened. Perhaps you would be good enough to bring back the blanket, slippers and gown in the morning?'

'Oh! Well, thank you. I'm a great nuisance, I'm afraid. Shall I take my clothes with me?'

'No, no. They are being washed and disinfected. You may collect them in the morning.'

Daisy avoided the doctor's eye. 'I'm sorry I've been so tiresome. I'm very grateful…'

Sister smiled. 'It is a common happening that people—and cars—should fall in the canals. You will come to no harm, I think.'

Mr der Huizma spoke. 'Shall we go, Miss Gillard?'

So Daisy, much hampered by the blanket and the too-large slippers, trotted beside him, out of the hospital, and was shoved neatly into the dark grey Rolls Royce outside.

It was a short drive, and beyond expressing the

polite hope that she would enjoy the rest of her stay in Amsterdam, he had nothing to say. And as for Daisy, it seemed to her it was hardly the occasion for casual conversation.

At the hotel he ushered her across the narrow pavement and into the foyer, where he engaged the proprietor in a brief conversation, not a word of which Daisy could understand. But presently he turned to her, expressed the hope that she was none the worse for her ducking, and bade her goodbye.

Daisy, at a disadvantage because of the blanket, thanked him again, untangled a hand from the blanket and offered it. His large, cool hand felt strangely comforting.

The next morning, her normal, neatly dressed self, not a hair out of place, she took a taxi to the hospital, handed over the blanket, the gown and the slippers in exchange for her own clothes, and made a short speech of thanks to Sister, who nodded and smiled, wished her a happy day and a safe return home and warned her to be careful.

There was no sign of Mr der Huizma, and there was no reason why there should have been; he was obviously a senior member of his profession who probably only went to Casualty when his skills were required. All the same, Daisy lingered for as long as possible in the hope of seeing him.

Mijnheer Friske had the wine cooler packed up

ready for her to take. She arranged to collect it that evening, when she went to get her train to the Hoek. It would be unwieldy, but no heavier than a big suitcase, and there would be porters and her father had said that he would see that she was met at Harwich. She assured Heer Friske that she would be back in good time, checked the contents of her handbag—ticket, passport, money and all the impedimenta necessary for her journey—and set off to spend the rest of the day window shopping, exploring the city and buying one or two small gifts.

Being a girl of common sense, she left her clothes, including those the hospital had returned to her, with the kindly Heer Friske, taking only her coat with her which she presently left at a dry cleaners to be collected later. Everything was going very smoothly, and she intended to enjoy her day.

And she did, cramming in as much as possible; another museum, a church or two, antique shops, browsing round the Bijnenkorf looking for presents.

It was late afternoon, after a cup of tea and an elaborate cream cake, when she started on her way back to Heer Friske's shop.

She walked through the narrow streets, thinking about her stay in Holland—a very enjoyable one, despite the ducking in a canal that had been the means of meeting Mr der Huizma again. Not quite the meeting she would have chosen. Aware of her lack of looks, she was sure that a soaking in canal water had done little to improve them. And there was nothing glamorous about a hospital blanket.

She was almost at Heer Friske's shop, walking down a narrow quiet street with no one to be seen, the houses lining it with doors and windows shut, when she was suddenly aware of danger. Too late, unfortunately. Someone snatched her handbag, and when she struggled to get it back someone else knocked her down. She hit the cobbles with a thump, was aware of a sudden terrible pain in her head, and was thankfully unconscious.

The two men disappeared as swiftly and silently as they had appeared. It was ten minutes or so before a man on a bicycle found her, and another ten minutes before an ambulance arrived to take her to hospital.

CHAPTER THREE

MR DER HUIZMA, leaving the hospital in the early morning after operating on a small baby with intussusception, met Casualty Sister in the foyer, also on her way home. He paused to wish her good morning, for they had known each other for some years, and enquired after her night.

'Busy—as busy as you, sir. By the way, the English girl is back…'

He paused in his stride. 'She was to return to England last night. What has happened to her?'

'Mugged. She was brought in about five o'clock. Concussion. No identification, of course—they took everything. They traced her name from the admissions book and notified the hotel. The proprietor couldn't give much information, only that she had paid her bill and intended to leave for England that evening.'

Mr der Huizma sighed and turned on his heel. 'Perhaps I can be of some assistance. Her father must be told…'

The sister of the ward to which Daisy had been taken was in her office. She got up as he came in. 'The English girl—we have tried to telephone her family but there was no reply…she is still unconscious, sir. You would wish to see her? Dr Brem is with her now.'

Daisy looked very neat lying in bed. Her hair had been plaited and lay on her pillow; her arms were neatly arranged on the coverlet. She was rather pale, and now and again she frowned.

Mr der Huizma nodded to his colleague. 'No fracture? No brain damage?'

'Not as far as we can see. Rather a deep concussion, but all her reflexes are normal. You've seen Sister?'

'Yes.' Mr der Huizma bent over the bed. 'Daisy, Daisy, can you hear me?'

The frown deepened, but she didn't open her eyes. She mumbled, 'Go away, I'm asleep.' And then added, 'My head aches.'

Mr der Huizma took a hand in his. 'My poor dear. You shall have something for that at once, and when you wake up you will feel better.'

He spoke very softly. 'Is your father meeting you at Harwich?'

'How else am I to get the wine cooler halfway across England? Go away.'

Which he did, to retire to Sister's office and pick up the phone.

Her father, waiting patiently for the ferry to dock, was surprised to hear his name on the loudspeaker.

'A phone call from Holland,' he was told, and was ushered into a small office to take it.

'Daisy?'

'Jules der Huizma, Mr Gillard. Daisy has had an accident. She is not seriously hurt but she has concussion. I have just come from her bedside and she has regained consciousness. She is being well cared for and I can assure you that you have no need for anxiety. She will be kept in hospital for a few days and I will personally arrange her return to you.'

'How did it happen?'

'She was mugged. Her handbag was taken, so it will be necessary for her to obtain a new passport and money. Someone will give her assistance with this.'

'Should I come over? Or my wife?'

'There is no need, unless you have a strong wish to do so. She must be kept quiet for a few days, and you would only be allowed to visit her for a brief period. I will phone you each day and let you know how she is getting on. One other thing—she spoke of a wine cooler. Is this something which can be dealt with?'

'Yes, yes. Heer Friske...I'll explain...'

When he'd finished, Mr der Huizma said, 'I'll see to the matter for you,' before bidding him a civil goodbye.

He went home then, wondering why he had saddled himself with offers of help to a comparative stranger. Heaven knew his days were busy enough, without hunting wine coolers and the self-imposed task of phoning Daisy's father each evening. He let himself into the tall narrow house which was his home, climbed the carved staircase at the end of the narrow hall, showered and dressed and went down to his breakfast.

He was met in his dining room by an elderly man, thin and stooping, with a severe expression, who wished him good morning and observed in accusing accents that Mr der Huizma had been out half the night again. 'It's not right,' he grumbled, 'having you out at all hours, and you an important man.'

Mr der Huizma, looking through his post, made light of it.

'It's my job, Joop, and I enjoy it.' He smiled at him. 'I'm famished…'

He had a busy day ahead of him, with no time to think about Daisy, but in the early evening on his way out of the hospital he went to see her.

She was having long periods of consciousness, Sister told him, and had obediently drunk the variety of beverages offered her. She had spoken very little.

'She seems worried about something called a wine cooler.'

'Ah, yes, that is something I can deal with on my

way home. I'd like to see her for a few minutes if that is convenient?'

Sister beamed at him—such a nice man, and always so courteous and thoughtful. She led the way to Daisy's bed and, being a sentimental woman, thought how charming she looked lying there quietly, her hair in a neat plait, her pale face devoid of make-up. She glanced at Mr der Huizma, wondering if he thought the same. He might be engaged to marry, but surely his heart would be touched...

Mr der Huizma, his heart quite untouched, looked down at Daisy with a professional eye. Dr Brem had assured him that she was doing nicely. A few days in bed and she would be perfectly fit.

And Daisy, looking back at him, could see that his look was wholly professional, not the friendly look of the nice man she had walked with on the beach at home. She said politely, 'Good evening, Mr der Huizma. I am quite recovered.'

'In a few more days,' he cautioned her. 'I am going to see Heer Friske this evening. Is there anything you wish me to say to him?'

'That's very kind of you. I expect he may be wondering why I haven't been to collect the wine cooler and my things. Would you please tell him that I'll come in a few days' time and get it, and take it home with me.'

'An awkward thing to travel with, surely?'

'Well, a bit, but I'll manage. Thank you for going to see him.' She frowned. 'How did you know about it?'

'Your father told me. I phoned to tell him that you were delayed and the reason for it.'

'Thank you. I'm sorry to be such a nuisance.'

'It is no trouble. I'm glad to see that you have recovered so well.' He smiled then. 'Sleep well.'

He turned away and then paused. 'I should have told you at once. Your mother and father know that you are quite safe and in good hands; they send their love. They would have come here but I said that there was no need, that you would be home again in a few days.'

When he had gone, Daisy closed her eyes and went over their conversation. It had been brief, impersonal, and he had been impatient under his perfect bedside manner. Probably he considered her a nuisance and would be glad to see the last of her. Her spirits, already at their lowest, sank without trace, and two tears rolled slowly down her cheeks. Before she could wipe them away Sister was by her bed, on her evening round.

'Daisy? In tears? Has Mr der Huizma upset you?'

'No, no. He's been most kind.' Daisy managed a smile. 'I've got a little headache…'

She swallowed tablets, drank a warm drink, assured everyone that she felt perfectly all right and closed her eyes. She didn't think she would sleep, but if she kept them shut Sister would report to the night staff that she was asleep. They were all so kind… It would be nice to be home again, and when she was she would forget Mr der Huizma.

Satisfactory arrangements having been made with Heer Friske, Mr der Huizma went home, remembering with a twinge of annoyance that he was dining with friends that evening and that his future bride would expect him to call for her so that they might arrive together. Before then he had a good deal to do; the post to read, phone calls to make, patients' notes to study.

He went to his study, closely followed by Joop with a tray of coffee and a small dog of nondescript appearance. He thanked Joop for the coffee, received delighted greetings from the dog and sat down behind his desk.

There were biscuits on the tray, which he offered the dog while he drank his coffee. 'I have to go out this evening, Bouncer. I do not particularly wish to do so. I am coming to the conclusion that I am not a socially minded man. When I return we will have a pleasant walk before bed.'

Bouncer hung out his tongue and panted, ate the last of the biscuits and made himself comfortable on his master's feet. He was a unique specimen of dog, as Mr der Huizma frequently told his friends. Long and thin in body, and covered with a silky coat, he possessed short legs and large ears. He had beautiful amber eyes and the heart of a lion. And he loved his master with an undemanding devotion. He closed his eyes now and dozed while Mr der Huizma opened the first of his letters.

Presently he got up and went through the house to let Bouncer out into the narrow walled garden behind it. It was a cold night, but the sky was clear and there was a frost. Walking up and down its length while Bouncer raced to and fro, Mr der Huizma found himself thinking of his walk along the shore in England. Daisy had been a good companion, saying little and when she did talking sense. He sighed for no reason at all, whistled to Bouncer, and went to dress for the evening.

Helene van Tromp, the lady who had every intention of marrying him, lived with her parents in a vast flat in the Churchillaan. She was hardly in the first flush of youth, being only a year or so younger than Mr der Huizma—and he had turned thirty-five—but she was considered a handsome woman by her friends; very fair, with large blue eyes, regular features and a fashionably slender figure, kept so, as only her dearest friends knew, by constant visits to her gym instructor and the beauty parlour. She was always exquisitely dressed, with never a hair out of place, and Mr der Huizma, arriving at her home, was given a cheek to kiss and told not to disarrange her hair.

'You're late,' she told him. 'I had hoped that we might have had a talk with Mother and Father; you see them so seldom.' She smiled enchantingly at him. 'Of course when we are married we shall be able to spend more time with them...'

'I shall be just as busy then as I am now,' he pointed out.

She gave a little laugh. 'Don't be silly, Jules. You can give up all that hospital work once we're married and build up your private practice. We shall have time and leisure to see more of our friends.'

Mr der Huizma thought privately that that was the last thing he wished to do; he had friends of his own, sober, married men with families and comfortable wives, as involved in their work as he was in his. He didn't particularly like Helene's friends, although he had done his best to do so, and he had thought in a vague way that once they were married she would take an interest in his friends and his work. It struck him forcibly now that that didn't seem likely. It seemed hardly the time to argue about it; he made his polite goodbyes to Helene's parents and drove with her to the dinner party.

'A wasted evening,' he told the faithful Bouncer much later, walking with him round the quiet streets near his house. There must be something wrong with him, since he had been unable to enjoy the light-hearted dinner table talk. Some of it had been malicious, and some of it had sparkled with wit, but no one there had said anything which meant anything. To be amused and amusing was all that was required.

It was some time later, as he was on his way up to bed, that he paused on the staircase to wonder why he had wanted to marry Helene and if he had ever been in love with her. It was a sobering thought to take to his bed. It should have kept him awake, but he was a tired man, and strangely enough it was Daisy's face which imposed itself upon his last waking moments.

Two days later Dr Brem pronounced Daisy fit to go home, and, meeting Mr der Huizma on his way into the hospital, told him.

'Not immediately?'

'No, no. She has arrangements to make, of course, but her new passport came today and she has received money for her journey. Another couple of days, I should think. You're going to see her again?'

'Yes. I'm off to Utrecht this evening, but I'll be back before she leaves.'

'Nice little thing,' said Dr Brem. 'We shall miss her—been no trouble at all.'

Daisy, setting about the business of getting herself and the wine cooler back home, wondered if Mr der

Huizma would come to see her again. By the end of the following day, all ready to leave the next morning, she had to admit that he wasn't coming. She had told Sister that she had arranged to leave on the night ferry, and when that lady had wanted to know where she intended to spend her day until then had said, not quite truthfully, that she would be with a friend of her father's.

'Well, take care,' said Sister the next day, and shook hands briskly. After all, Daisy was a grown woman, and able to look after herself—despite her regrettable way of encountering accidents.

Ten minutes after Daisy left the hospital, Mr der Huizma parked his car in its forecourt, went to have a word with his registrar and then to see Daisy.

'She left not half an hour ago,' Sister told him. 'Dr Brem told her she could go home, though he advised her to stay another day or two. But she had everything arranged within a day—said she wanted to get back to England. She's going over on the night ferry.'

'It's only eleven o'clock in the morning,' Mr der Huizma pointed out.

'Yes, I know. I asked her what she intended doing all day and she said she would spend it with a friend of her father's.'

Mr der Huizma had a moment's regret for the

pleasant free day he had planned for himself. Daisy would most certainly go to collect the wretched wine cooler, and he had a fleeting vision of her transporting it and herself back to England. And probably having another accident…

When he went into Heer Friske's shop, he was standing on one side of the wine cooler, now wrapped in sacking and stout cardboard, and Daisy was on the other side. They both looked round as he went in. Heer Friske said nothing, but Daisy said, 'Oh', in an annoyed voice.

Undeterred by this cool reception, Mr der Huizma crossed the small shop to join them.

'Wondering what on earth to do with it?' he asked cheerfully.

Daisy shot him a cold look. 'Certainly not. All my arrangements are made.'

Mr der Huizma glanced at Heer Friske, who shrugged his shoulders. 'Miss Gillard is happy to take the wine cooler with her—who am I to stop her?'

Mr der Huizma smiled a little. 'I am travelling to England by the midnight ferry from the Hoek,' he said smoothly. 'I shall be happy to take Miss Gillard and the wine cooler in the car with me.'

'Quite unnecessary,' said Daisy quickly. 'Thank you all the same. I'm quite able to travel as I have already planned.'

'Oh, I'm sure of that. I have no doubt you are capable of doing anything you wish, but why be pig-headed about it? It's of no consequence to me if you come or not; I'm merely making a practical suggestion.'

He didn't wait for her answer. While she was seeking one he nodded again at Heer Friske, who picked up the wine cooler and carried it out of the shop.

'Where is he taking it?'

Daisy started after him, but somehow Mr der Huizma was in the way.

'To my car. Be sensible, Daisy.'

'That's all very well, but I don't know where you're taking it.'

'We will take it to my house, where you will remain as my guest until it is time to leave for the ferry.' He sounded so reasonable.

'Indeed I won't,' said Daisy roundly. 'Whatever next? You must have no wish to have me as a guest, and what about your wife…?'

'I am not married,' said Mr der Huizma mildly, 'and I can't think why you should imagine that I don't want you as a guest. I don't remember ever saying so.'

He uttered this in such matter-of-fact tones that she believed him. 'Well, it's very kind of you.'

'Not at all. We will go to my home now, and if

you wish to spend the day shopping or sightseeing, feel free to do so. Although perhaps it would be sensible if you were to lunch with me so that we can discuss the journey. We shall need to leave soon after eight o'clock this evening.'

She found herself on the pavement outside the shop, watching Heer Friske stowing the wine cooler and her suitcase in the boot of the Rolls, and presently, after suitable goodbyes had been exchanged she was in the car, sitting beside a silent Mr der Huizma.

It wasn't an unpleasant silence, rather she found it reassuring, so that she allowed her thoughts to simmer gently without bothering her too much. It had all happened rather quickly, and soon she would probably have second thoughts, but of course by then it would be too late to do anything. Besides, the wine cooler was in the car, and getting it out again would present a problem even if she decided to change her mind. Upon rather dreamy reflection about this, she decided that it would be foolish to do that.

Mr der Huizma drew up before his house, got out of the car and opened her door. She stood for a moment on the pavement and looked up at it. It was very old, in a row of old houses each with a different gable, their windows gleaming, their paintwork pristine. She mounted the stone steps beside him and the heavy old door with its handsome transom was opened as they reached it.

Mr der Huizma, who usually let himself into his home, hid a smile. He bade Joop good morning in his own language and turned to Daisy. 'This is Joop, who runs my home with his wife, Jette. He speaks English, and if I am not around he will help you in any way.

'Miss Gillard will be travelling over to England with me this evening, Joop. On the night ferry.'

Joop's severe expression didn't alter. 'Very good, *mijnheer*. I will bring coffee to the drawing room. If Miss Gillard would like to come with me, I will fetch Jette.'

Mr der Huizma had picked up a pile of letters from the console table against one wall and was leafing through them. 'Yes, do that, Joop.' He nodded at Daisy. 'See you in five minutes or so, Daisy. Joop will show you where to go.'

Daisy was handed over to a stout middle-aged woman with a round cheerful face and small dark eyes who trotted her off to a cloakroom tucked away at the end of a long hallway, smiled and nodded, and shut the door on her. Daisy tidied her already tidy person, peered for a brief moment in the mirror and decided that she looked plainer than usual, then went into the hall again to find Jette waiting for her. She in turn handed her over to Joop, who led the way back down the hall to a pair of splendid double doors which he opened with all the pomp one would have expected for the entrance of the fairy queen.

Daisy slipped past him and stood for a moment looking around her. The room appeared empty except for a small, unusual-looking dog who came to meet her, looking pleased.

Daisy stooped to pat him. 'What a splendid fellow you are,' she told him, and advanced a few steps into the room. It was large and high ceilinged, with two tall windows draped in claret velvet curtains. There was a scattering of comfortable chairs and small tables, a very beautiful rent table between the windows, and two display cabinets on either side of the great fireplace. Daisy, her small nose twitching with interest, took a few more steps.

'Eighteen-century marquetry and in perfect condition,' she informed the dog.

She squeaked with surprise when Mr der Huizma observed, 'Quite right. Rather nice, aren't they?'

He had been standing in a doorway at the end of the room, watching her, and added, 'I see Bouncer has made friends. You like dogs?'

'Yes, yes, I do. I'm sorry—I didn't mean to pry.'

'Hardly that, surely. Now if you had opened one of the cabinets and taken out some of the contents I might possibly have taken umbrage.'

Daisy said. 'You speak such good English. I

mean, you use words which quite a few English people don't often use.'

'Thank you, Daisy. That is probably because I'm a Dutchman. Here's Joop with the coffee. Come and sit over here and decide what you wish to do with your day.'

'Don't you have to work?'

She chose a small armchair covered in tapestry and Bouncer came and sat at her feet.

'No. I have been in Utrecht. Now I have a day or so free.'

She poured coffee from a very beautiful little silver coffee pot. Early eighteenth century? she thought. And the cups and saucers—fine, paper-thin porcelain. She handled them delicately and supposed it would be rude if she were to ask about them.

'The coffee pot is 1625 and the cups and saucers are later—around seventeen-hundred.'

'They're very lovely. Are you not afraid of breaking them?'

'No. They are in constant use. Jette doesn't allow anyone else to wash them but herself.'

'So many people hide their treasures away in cupboards…'

'In which case they might just as well be smashed. Have one of these biscuits—Jette is a splendid cook.'

Daisy drank the delicious coffee and ate the biscuits. She felt that she should be feeling awkward or annoyed at having her plans changed so ruthlessly—or even shy…but she felt remarkably at ease. In fact, she was enjoying herself…

Presently Mr der Huizma begged to be excused while he saw to his letters and made some phone calls. 'If you don't wish to go out, feel free to do what you want here. There's a library across the hall, with books and papers and magazines, and if you would like, Joop will show you the door into the garden.'

'A garden? Here behind the house? I'd like to see it, if it's not a bother.'

'Joop shall take you to the garden door.'

She was led through a narrow door beside the staircase, down a couple of steps and along a paved passage. The house went back a long way from the street, with windows in the oddest places. When Joop opened the door onto the garden she could see that although it was narrow it was a good length. Beautifully laid out, too, with narrow brick paths on either side of a small lawn and on either side of the paths flowerbeds backing onto high brick walls. She walked down to the end and found a little arbour and a small pond with a fountain—not running water, of course. The pond was sheltered by a trellis of roses.

In summer it would be a delightful place in which to sit and do nothing, reflected Daisy, and despite the chilly day she sat down in the arbour. This was a lovely house. She corrected herself—a lovely home. A grand house, splendidly furnished, but lived in and loved. When Mr der Huizma married—and of course he would—his wife would be the happiest woman on earth. Daisy, quite carried away, started to daydream aloud.

'Fancy sitting here on a summer's day. There would be a baby in a pram, and two or three children running around, and Bouncer, and perhaps a cat and kittens…'

Mr der Huizma, pausing on the path to listen to this, observed mildly, 'It sounds delightful, but surely rather crowded?'

Daisy felt a fool. 'I was just pretending. Don't you ever pretend?'

'Not enough. I must cultivate the habit. Do you like my garden?'

'It's perfect.'

'Come with me; I'll show you something.' He took her to an ancient door in the end wall, drew its bolts, turned its great key, and opened it. Outside there was a paved space, and beyond that a canal. There were steps too, and at the bottom of them a small boat.

'Your back door?' hazarded Daisy, and, when he nodded, 'Of course, long ago it must have been a sort of tradesman's entrance. What a splendid idea. Do you use it?'

'Seldom—although when I was a small boy I used to row myself out into the main canals.'

Daisy stared at the still dark water. 'Your mother must have been terrified.'

'So she has frequently told me.'

She wanted to ask him about his boyhood, his mother, his family, but instead she asked how far away the main canal was, and listened intelligently when he explained.

They went back into the garden presently, and then into the house to sit in his lovely drawing room and sip sherry and talk about any number of things.

Daisy, her tongue loosened by the sherry, her annoyance forgotten, told him a good deal more about herself than she realised, and Mr der Huizma, enjoying himself, egged her on.

They lunched in a rather grand dining room, with a rectangular table, lovely ribbon-backed chairs, a massive side-table and family portraits on its panelled walls. Daisy, undeterred by the ancestors looking down upon her, ate her toast and pâté, scrambled eggs and smoked salmon, and thin slices of cheese with croissants warm in their basket, drank the coffee Joop offered her, and then, at her host's suggestion, followed him into the library.

A smallish dim room, lined with bookshelves, with a large leather-covered table ringed by comfortable chairs—and a set of George the Third library steps, which her professional eye lighted upon with interest.

There were books in abundance, and the table was covered with newspapers, magazines and a variety of journals; she could have spent the day there very happily. She roamed round while Mr der Huizma settled himself into a chair, waiting patiently until she had had her fill. Only then did he get up.

'I've a history of this house. Would you like to see it?'

'Oh, yes, please. Is it a first edition?'

'Yes, and written in Dutch, but some of the drawings are interesting.'

They were bending over it, Daisy absorbed while he translated from the Dutch, when the door was opened. He looked up and said, 'Why, Helene, this is a surprise,' and crossed the room to meet the woman who had entered.

Daisy had looked up too. Here was the living image of what she so longed to be. Perfection, no less—tall, blonde and beautiful, dressed exquisitely with simple elegance, slim as a wand. Daisy added the thought that she was *too* thin, bony in fact. Just a little more shape would have made her quite perfect. Perhaps, thought Daisy, Mr der Huizma liked very thin women.

She glanced down at her own well-rounded person and sighed.

Mr der Huizma was speaking. 'Daisy, come and meet Helene van Tromp—my fiancée.' He had a hand on Helene's arm. 'Helene, this is Daisy Gillard, who has been here dealing with the buying and selling of antiques—she is an expert.'

Daisy offered a hand and smiled. Helene smiled too, only the smile didn't reach her eyes. 'How interesting. Have you bought something from this house? I do hope so; I dislike all this old furniture.'

Daisy said in a shocked voice, 'But no one would want to sell anything in this house; it's full of treasures.'

Helene looked at Mr der Huizma. 'So why is she here?'

'Daisy is here because I am giving her a lift back to England on the night ferry.'

Helene, for a split second, didn't look beautiful. 'Oh?' She glanced at Daisy. 'Did you fall under Jules's car or faint on his doorstep?'

Daisy said matter-of-factly, 'No, nothing like that. I fell in a canal and Mr der Huizma hauled me out and took me to the hospital. Oh, and then I got mugged. He heard that I was going back to England today and offered me a lift, that's all!'

Helene stared at her for a moment, and then smiled. A dull girl, with no looks to speak of, and obviously she hadn't succumbed to Jules's charm, nor was she impressed by his obvious wealth. Daisy was dismissed as not worth bothering about.

Mr der Huizma was called away then, to take an urgent phone call, and Helene seized her chance. 'You must be tired,' she said sweetly. 'Why don't you go and have a rest? You have a long journey before you.'

She took Daisy's arm, led her to the door and opened it. 'There's a small sitting room no one uses; you can curl up on a sofa and have a nap. I'll tell Joop to bring you a cup of tea later.'

Daisy wasn't in the least tired, but it was obvious that Helene wanted to get rid of her—which in all fairness was quite understandable. Daisy supposed that if she were engaged to someone like Mr der Huizma she would want to keep him to herself. She allowed herself to be drawn across the hall and into another room.

'No one will disturb you,' said Helene softly, and shut the door on her.

The room was, comparatively speaking, small. It was also delightfully cosy, with comfortable chairs, a little writing desk and a round table upon which was a bowl of flowers. It was pleasantly warm too, and Daisy sat down in one of the chairs and looked around her. Helene had said it was a room which was seldom used, but it seemed to her to be very lived in. There were books scattered around, and magazines, but she didn't bother with them; she had plenty to occupy her thoughts.

She didn't like Helene, for a start, which seemed unkind considering how gracious that lady had been. She didn't think that Mr der Huizma would be happy with her, despite her beauty and elegance. It was no concern of hers, though. And probably they were ideally suited; Helene would undoubtedly grace this lovely old house and be a perfect hostess. Her thoughts became rather muddled with worrying about the wine cooler and how she was to get home once they reached England. She really should have settled the matter before agreeing to go with Mr der Huizma, although, come to think of it, she hadn't been given the opportunity…

Joop came presently with a tray of tea, enquiring if her headache was better and if there was anything she required. Daisy, who hadn't got a headache, thanked him politely and said, 'No, thank you.'

She drank her tea and wondered how long she should stay in the room—until they left that evening? Was she to have her dinner on a tray as well?

Questions which were answered by Mr der Huizma, who came in quietly and sat down opposite her.

'You must forgive me. I had no idea that you had a headache and were feeling tired.'

Daisy spoke without thinking. 'Oh, but I'm not in

the least tired, and my head doesn't ache. Helene—you don't mind me calling her that?—was kind enough to suggest that I might like to rest for a bit.'

She wasn't sure if she liked the look on his face, but he said pleasantly, 'In that case shall we have a drink before dinner?'

'That would be lovely. I like this room.'

'My mother uses it when she visits me...'

Daisy smiled. 'There, I had a feeling that it was lived in, if you know what I mean—writing letters and sewing and knitting, and just being happy.'

He looked at her thoughtfully. 'You are quite right, of course.'

They had their drinks, and presently dined, and then Daisy was led away by Jette so that she could get ready for the journey. The wine cooler was checked, her case put into the boot, and she herself stowed neatly in the car. Such luxury, thought Daisy happily, and then wondered not so happily if she would need to sustain a conversation all the way to the Hoek.

She need not have worried. Beyond making sure that she was comfortable, Mr der Huizma seemed happy enough with his thoughts; his austere profile certainly discouraged small talk.

CHAPTER FOUR

AFTER a while Daisy discovered that the silence between them was a restful one; the kind of silence between old friends who had no need to talk. She gave a small sigh of content and allowed her thoughts to wander. Father would be pleased about the cooler. Getting it from Harwich might be a bit difficult, but at least she would be back in England. Perhaps it would be a good idea to phone him and ask him to drive up to Harwich and collect her and it. It struck her then that she hadn't thought about that before, and Mr der Huizma had been a bit arbitrary, hadn't he? Still, never look a gift horse in the mouth. The most difficult part of the journey would be over by the time they got to Harwich.

At the Hoek he bade her stay in the car in a pleasant voice which none the less brooked no argument. He was gone for some time and she began to get uneasy. Just as she was wondering if she should go and look for him, he reappeared.

'We can go on board,' he told her.

'I haven't shown anyone my ticket...'

'I have tickets. You can cash yours in when we get to Harwich.'

'And pay you back,' said Daisy smartly, not wishing to be beholden.

'As you wish.' He had joined the queue of cars going aboard, and presently she found herself being urged up the stairs to the deck above. She would have paused here, but he told her, 'The top deck,' and led the way, carrying her overnight bag.

It was quiet there, with only a stewardess in sight to lead them to their cabins. Mr der Huizma nodded briefly as the woman opened a door. 'I'll see you in the restaurant in ten minutes,' he said and went on down the corridor to his own cabin.

Daisy looked around her. The cabin was small but very comfortable. First class, she supposed and wondered how much it would cost. And where was the restaurant? And supposing she hadn't wanted to go to it?

She brushed her mousy hair smooth, did her face and sat down on the bed. The ten minutes was already up but she really didn't see why she should go to the restaurant if she didn't want to. The trouble was, she did want to. She was hungry, for one thing, and for another, despite his silence, she quite liked being with Mr der Huizma.

He was there, waiting for her, very much at ease, coming to meet her as she hesitated in the doorway.

'A drink? It might be a good idea as the crossing is sometimes rough at this time of year.'

'Thank you,' said Daisy. 'It was quite rough when I crossed with the screen, but I wasn't sick.'

His thin mouth twitched slightly. 'How about a dry sherry? And it is always a good idea to have a meal.'

They ate presently, talking a little about one thing and another, never once mentioning her stay in Amsterdam, and as soon as their meal was finished Daisy said that she would like to go to her cabin.

He made no attempt to keep her. 'We dock around seven o'clock. Someone will bring you some tea and toast about half past six. We'll have breakfast later.' He didn't give her the chance to say anything but bade her goodnight abruptly. This question of breakfast would have to be settled in the morning. Once they were at Harwich she would collect the wine cooler and find somewhere quiet, phone her father and do whatever he thought best.

It was going to be a rough crossing. She got into her narrow bed feeling squeamish, but she was tired too; she was asleep before she could decide whether she felt seasick or not.

She was awakened by the stewardess with tea and toast and warned that the ferry would be docking shortly. 'A nasty rough crossing,' said the stewardess.

Certainly the ferry was still rolling around, making dressing a lengthy business, but the tea and toast stayed down and she felt her usual self. Finding her way on deck, she wondered if Mr der Huizma had slept too, and decided that he had. Somehow she couldn't associate him with being sick…

She saw him at once, leaning over the rail watching the ferry edging its way into the harbour. But he must have had eyes at the back of his head, for he turned round to look at her as she crossed the deck.

There was something about her, he reflected, which intrigued him. Certainly not her looks, although she had a delightful smile and her eyes were lovely; large and sparkling and… He sought for a word—kind. Helene had dismissed her as a dull girl, badly dressed and too reserved, but he knew that wasn't true. There was nothing dull about Daisy, and although her clothes were off the peg they were in good taste and she wore them with elegance. He found himself wishing that he knew more about her.

He went to meet her and they stood together watching the quay getting nearer. Presently they went down to the car deck and got into the Rolls. There would be a short delay before they could disembark; the opportunity Daisy was hoping for.

'If you wouldn't mind letting me get out once we are through Customs—and the wine cooler, of course?'

'And then what will you do, Daisy?' he wanted to know.

'Phone Father…'

'I phoned him yesterday before we left. I'm driving you home—you and your wine cooler.'

She turned to look at him. 'But it's miles; you can't possibly do that.'

'I'm spending the night with friends—remember I have stayed with them before? When we went walking on the shore?'

'Oh, well. That would be nice. Why didn't you tell me before?'

'Because I rather think that you would have flatly refused to come.'

She considered this. 'Yes, I think that perhaps I might have.' She smiled at him. 'But I'm really glad to have a lift all the way home. Thank you.'

'Don't thank me. I'm glad of the company.'

'Are you really? But you don't talk. I thought you were annoyed at having to offer me a lift.'

'Not at all, Daisy. But you are not a girl who expects to be entertained with small talk, are you?'

'No. And I don't mind if you don't say a word. There's always such a lot to think about.'

Mr der Huizma glanced at her and agreed gravely. He had a lot to think about too.

They were through Customs and on the way to Colchester when he suggested that they might stop for breakfast. He took her to Le Brasserie and they ate a splendid breakfast before going on to

Chelmsford, Brentwood and the ring road. The M25 was busy as he skirted round the north of the city to join the M3, and presently the A303. 'I'll turn off at Salisbury,' he told her.

They stopped at Fleet for coffee, and took the A303. There wasn't a great deal of traffic now that they were well away from London, and Mr der Huizma drove fast, saying little, leaving Daisy to look out at the wintry landscape. Once he had turned off to Salisbury she allowed her excitement at coming home to take over. She hadn't been away for long, but such a lot had happened; it would be nice to settle down to her usual quiet life. At least, she amended, for a time. Her visit to Amsterdam had given her a taste for foreign travel…

Once through Salisbury Mr der Huizma slowed the car's pace and Daisy gave him an enquiring look. They still had a long way to go. Surely it would have been quicker to keep to the A303?

'Lunch,' he told her briefly. 'There's a good restaurant just before we rejoin the A303.'

He stopped in a smallish village and turned in through the open gates of a large house in its centre. Inside there was a welcoming fire in the bar and a pretty dining room. Daisy sighed with pleasure and went off to the Ladies, then rejoined him at the bar to drink sherry and peruse the menu.

The food was excellent. There were other people

lunching, just enough to make the place feel cosy, and the log fire made nonsense of the cold grey day. And Mr der Huizma, abandoning his silence, became once again the man who had been such a pleasant companion walking along the shore…

They drove on then, turning off before Exeter and making for the coast through narrow Devon lanes.

'Mother will be delighted to give you tea,' said Daisy as he turned the car into the country road which would lead to her home.

'That is very kind, but I should get on. I shall be staying with my friends for a couple of days.'

Daisy blushed, for he had spoken in his usual quiet manner but she sensed a snub. She had been silly; of course he wouldn't want to stay for tea. He had given her a lift home but that was no reason to suppose that he would wish to take the matter further. She said, 'Yes, of course,' in a wooden voice, and added the remark that it would soon be dark.

Mr der Huizma had seen the blush and had a very good idea of what Daisy was thinking. He need not have been quite so brusque; indeed, he would have enjoyed meeting her father again, and her mother, and he had to admit that he regretted that he wouldn't see Daisy again. Which was a good thing, he reminded himself. He was beginning to find her too interesting…

The main street of the little town was deserted

when he stopped outside the antiques shop. The window was still lighted, and the door was opened at once and Mr Gillard came out to the car.

Mr der Huizma got out and opened Daisy's door, and stood quietly while Daisy was hugged and exclaimed over. But then Mr Gillard turned to him and wrung his hand. 'So good of you,' he declared, 'we are so grateful. Come along in—there's tea waiting.'

Mr der Huizma gave a mental shrug. Another half-hour of Daisy's company would do no harm. After all he would never see her again. He followed the older man into the shop.

Daisy had run upstairs to her mother. 'It's so lovely to be home,' she declared. 'And I've such a lot to tell you…'

She broke off as her father and Mr der Huizma came into the room and smiled widely at him, because he had changed his mind after all. And he, seeing the smile, wished very much that their paths would not lie so far apart. He had a fleeting image of Helene then, reminding him that such a wish was something he must forget.

They had tea, and he sat by Mrs Gillard, answering her questions about Daisy, assuring her that no harm had been done and then telling Mr Gillard about Heer Friske and the wine cooler—which remark led easily enough to a brief chat about antiques. And all the time Daisy sat quietly, saying very little, wishing that time would stand still so that Mr der Huizma could stay for ever.

But of course it didn't. Presently he got up, thanked her mother for his tea, offered to unload the wine cooler and then shook Daisy's hand and wished her goodbye too, in a friendly voice devoid of warmth.

Then he had gone.

Daisy started to clear away the tea things and her mother went to the window to watch their guest drive away. 'A lovely car,' she observed, 'and what a very nice man, love. I suppose his being a doctor makes him have such beautiful manners.'

Daisy said that, yes, she supposed so, in such a quiet voice that her mother gave her a quick glance and added, 'Well, you'll be able to tell us all about it this evening, dear. You run along and unpack your things and I'll see about supper. You must have a great deal to tell us.'

And indeed Daisy spent the rest of the evening giving a faithful account of her stay in Holland, making much over the delivery of the screen and her visits to Heer Friske, but glossing over her encounters with Mr der Huizma.

Mr der Huizma, dining with his friends that evening, told them his version of his various encounters with Daisy. 'You didn't mind my coming at such short notice? I knew Daisy from my previous visit—you remember that hotel where we dined together? We met there, and as you know I saw her several times while I was staying here. I felt that the least I could do was to see her safely back home with this wine cooler.'

His hostess said gently, 'Poor girl, falling in the canal and then being mugged. Such a nice sensible girl too. She is very well liked, you know, but funnily enough as far as I know she hasn't any boyfriends. Of course young men want pretty faces…'

It was at breakfast the following morning that Mr der Huizma was asked by his hostess if a date had been set for his wedding.

'Helene is in no hurry to marry; she leads a busy social life—she will be going to Switzerland to ski, and then some friends of hers have invited her to go to California.'

His host chipped in. 'A pity. I don't suppose Gillard told you last night—he's not a man to boast—but when I was there last week he showed me a really beautiful diamond brooch—a perfect bow—just the kind of gift a bridegroom would give his bride. Funnily enough I thought of your Helene—such a beautiful woman. He bought it from the Lancey-Courtneys; they've been selling a good deal of stuff lately. It belonged to a great-great-grandmother, I believe, and no one in the family liked it.' He chuckled. 'I was tempted to mortgage this house and buy it for Grace.' He smiled at his wife. 'But she persuaded me not to.'

Mr der Huizma passed his cup for more coffee. 'It sounds exactly the kind of thing Helene would like to have. Perhaps I'd better take a look at it.'

It would mean seeing Daisy again. He smiled at the thought…

Daisy, tying price tickets on a collection of small china figures, looked round at the tinkle of the door-bell. Her father was in his office, she had slipped back into her accustomed routine, and already Amsterdam seemed a dream. The sight of Mr der Huizma, wandering through the crowded shop towards her, made the dream reality. She put down the china ornament, aware that her hand wasn't quite steady, but she wished him good morning in a normal voice.

His good morning was friendly. 'Busy already, Daisy? Do you not take a holiday from time to time?'

'Well, going to Holland was like a holiday. Do you want to see Father?'

'I've been told he has a brooch I would like to see…'

She fetched her father then, and went back to her pricing, and the two men went into the office. She wondered why; perhaps her journey home had cost more than her ticket, and then there had been their meals. Her father would probably insist on paying for them. But why should Mr der Huizma come to the shop? She was sure her father hadn't suggested it on the previous evening.

The office door opened and her father called, 'Daisy, come here, will you?'

The two men were standing at his desk, looking down at the brooch lying in its bed of dark blue velvet. It shone and sparkled and she said involuntarily, 'Oh, what a pretty thing.'

Her father touched it with a gentle finger. 'Yes, it is. It's also very dirty.' He glanced at Mr der Huizma. 'I couldn't let you have it in this state. When did you want it?'

Mr der Huizma's voice sounded remote. 'It is to be a wedding gift to my bride. There is no great hurry, however, we are unlikely to marry before the summer. But I should like to buy it.' He paused, and the sudden idea in his head became vital action. 'I shall be returning home later today, but may I leave it with you to clean? I see no chance of coming this way for some time, though. Perhaps Daisy could bring it over when it is ready?' He smiled suddenly. 'She has proved herself a splendid custodian for the screen and the wine cooler, and the brooch wouldn't be difficult to transport.'

'Well, I don't see why she shouldn't do that. The brooch will take some time to clean—a couple of weeks...'

The two men looked at Daisy, Mr der Huizma with his eyebrows gently raised, her father fondly. She saw that she was supposed to say something.

'Yes, of course I'll take it,' said Daisy, and at the same moment Mr der Huizma knew that nothing on earth would allow him to let Daisy travel alone with the brooch—she could be mugged again, injured. He realised that the brooch didn't matter, but Daisy did. Behind his placid features his clever head was already full of half-formed plans.

But for the moment he said nothing. Ways and means were discussed, and presently the two men went upstairs to talk over the idea with coffee. Daisy stayed in the shop and sold a pair of brass candlesticks and a copper bed-warmer to a young American couple honeymooning in England. She let them have the bed-warmer for less than the price on the ticket because they were so obviously happy and delighted with their purchases.

She felt happy too. She hadn't allowed herself to dwell too much on the fact that she wouldn't see Mr der Huizma again, but she had been aware of disappointment, almost sadness at the thought. But now she would go to Amsterdam again, and even if their meeting was brief, it would mean that she would see him once more. Their paths had crossed several times, she reminded herself, and she had come to regard him as a friend. She thought of the brooch then—a splendid gift for his Helene. 'If I were Helene,' muttered Daisy to the empty shop, 'I'd be head over heels in love with him.'

When he and her father came back into the shop she was buying a small Wedgwood teapot from an elderly lady. A genuine piece, with the model of the widow on its lid, and worth a good deal more than the lady had asked for it. By the time she had paid the delighted owner its true value, Mr der Huizma had gone…

The task of cleaning the brooch fell to her lot; she had patience with finicky jobs and she spent part of each day restoring it to its original sparkle, so that she was constantly reminded of Helene and Mr der Huizma. She didn't hurry over it. There was no need, her father had pointed out, and besides the shop had to be attended to if he was busy elsewhere. A week went by, and a second, and midway through the third week the brooch was ready. Minutely examined by her father and carefully packed up. Any day now, as soon as it was convenient, she would go over to Holland. Or so she thought!

Back in Amsterdam Mr der Huizma had immediately immersed himself in his work, and only some days following his return did he visit Helene.

'So you're back again,' she greeted him. 'Really, Jules, you must cut down on your work. Give up some of the hospitals where you have beds. Oh, I know you need to keep your hand in with the children on the wards, but you would have a far bigger private practice if you did. There are plenty of other doctors who could take over from you…'

She was looking very beautiful that evening, beautifully dressed and made up and ready to charm him.

But he discovered that he wasn't charmed. He was fair enough to realise that he did spend many of his days and quite often his nights with his small patients, but Helene had known that when she had said that she would marry him. He saw now that she had no real interest in his work; she would cavil at interrupted meals, broken nights and urgent flights to other countries, she would be quite unable to visualise the kind of life they would lead together, and certainly she wouldn't be willing to give up the social round which was so important to her.

But he was an honourable man. He had asked her to marry him believing that he had loved her. He *had* been in love with her, but that wasn't enough and that wasn't her fault…

He said now, 'Helene, my work is my life. My patients matter to me—if you were to come to the hospital and see some of the little ones you would understand that.'

Helene crossed the room and sat down beside him on the sofa. 'You're tired because you're working too hard. Of course you enjoy your profession, it must be most interesting, but why wear yourself out? Life's too short. I've been invited to fly down to Cannes for a week—the van Hoffmans. Come with me; they told me to bring you if you were free.'

'But I'm not free,' said Mr der Huizma quietly.

Helene frowned. 'Nonsense. Really, Jules, you're deliberately annoying me…'

'No, Helene.' He sounded tired and remote, and she had a sudden feeling that she had gone too far. She didn't love him, but he would suit her as a husband—money, an old family, making a name for himself in his profession. She had thought that her future was secure with him, but now she felt a faint prickle of doubt. She laid a hand on his arm.

'Don't be angry, Jules. I do know how much your work means to you, but I worry that you don't have enough leisure.'

He went home presently, and sat for a long time in his study with the faithful Bouncer for company. He saw nothing but unhappiness for himself and Helene if they were to marry. He was aware that she didn't love him, had never even *been* in love with him, but she had seemed so suitable.

'I'm a fool,' said Mr der Huizma to Bouncer, who wagged his tail and whined in sympathy. It was late when he at last went up to bed. The half-formed plans he had allowed to simmer at the back of his head had resolved themselves. Tomorrow he would go and see Heer Friske.

It was early evening before he reached the antiques shop. His day had been long, and there were several sick children who were concerning him. He was tired, but this was something he had promised himself he would do.

The shop was still open, and when he walked in Heer Friske came to meet him.

'The wine cooler has arrived safely; I have heard from Mr Gillard. It was good of you to give Daisy a lift back, *mijnheer*.'

'It was no trouble. It would have been an awkward journey for her by ferry and train, although she seems a sensible young woman.'

'Indeed, and a knowledgeable one too. She has the instincts of a good antiques dealer. I dare say she will find work with one of the big firms in London…'

This was the opening Mr der Huizma sought. 'She is most interested in Dutch antiques. Did she not tell you? But of course she doesn't know anyone in Holland who would train her…'

'She knows me,' observed Heer Friske. 'I

wouldn't mind having her for a couple of months. The tourist season will be starting shortly, and I was thinking of getting someone.'

Mr der Huizma murmured in a disinterested voice and went to look at an attractive small enamel box, a pretty trifle, pale green and painted with roses. He bought it without speaking of Daisy again, and presently went home. Perhaps nothing would come of it, but Heer Friske had risen to his bait.

And Heer Friske was thinking about it, pondering the pros and cons. He decided that he would write to Mr Gillard.

He was a cautious old man, and he deliberated over the matter for some time and then finally wrote his letter.

Mr Gillard read it several mornings later over his breakfast. He read it twice before remarking, 'This letter will be of interest to you, Daisy. Heer Friske asks if you would like to work for him for a short period. He was impressed by your knowledge of antiques and thinks that a month or so in his shop will broaden it.'

Mr Gillard took off his spectacles and looked at Daisy. 'You will do as you wish, of course, but if my opinion is asked then I would say that it is a good idea. One can never know enough, and although you have no qualifications there is no reason why you shouldn't carry on here when I retire.'

'You're not going to retire for years,' said Daisy, 'but I see what you mean.'

She had a mental picture of herself in middle age, plain of face, slightly dowdy as to dress, and absorbed in her work. Well, there wouldn't be anything or anyone else to be absorbed in, would there? No husband or children, dogs, cats or ponies, all living in a comfortable house as happy as the day is long…

She brought her thoughts back to the present. She would like to go to Amsterdam, and not only for the reasons her father had mentioned. She would be in the same town as Mr der Huizma, she might meet him again, which was something she very much wanted to do.

'Yes, Father, I should like to go. When does Heer Friske want me to start?'

'He doesn't say. He writes that he will wait for your decision before he goes into details. I suppose it will be fairly soon, for the tourists will be arriving in Holland to see the bulb fields and I believe he does good business at that time.'

'I don't speak Dutch,' said Daisy.

'Well, probably most of his customers are American or English. You will be an asset in the shop. Of course, there is a good deal to discuss before you agree. Are you to be paid, I wonder, and what free time can you expect and where will you live?'

Her mother said quietly, 'Surely all that can be sorted out in one letter? And of course Heer Friske isn't going into details until he knows that Daisy will go to Amsterdam.' She added, 'You'll need some new clothes, dear.'

Something elegant, thought Daisy, so that Mr der Huizma would notice her—that was if they should meet…

Heer Friske was pleased at her decision; she would receive a small salary, he wrote, and commission on anything she might sell from his shop. She would be free on Sundays and Mondays, but on her working days she was not to expect any time off. She would have a room in his house; he and his wife would be glad to have her company. The date of her arrival was to be arranged within the next week or so.

Daisy took herself off to Plymouth. Spring might be in the air but it was still chilly. She bought a jacket and skirt in a warm brown tweed, a couple of woolly jumpers and a sober grey dress suitable for the shop. And, since her father had been generous with a cheque, she bought a three-piece in dark green jersey just in case she should encounter a social occasion.

She went back home, tried everything on before

packing them tidily, and waited to see what would happen next.

Mr der Huizma had allowed ten days or so to elapse before calling in at Heer Friske's shop once more. This time he bought an antique baby's rattle—coral and silver bells; it would doubtless make a handsome christening present for some baby or other later on. While he was purchasing it Heer Friske, in an unusually expansive mood, told him that he had engaged Daisy.

'That was a good idea of yours,' he observed, 'and it seemed worth asking her. She is glad to come, and I shall teach her all I can while she is here. She has her future to consider—probably she will take over her father's shop in due course. A nice girl, but not pretty, and unlikely to marry.'

'When is she to come?' enquired Mr der Huizma idly.

'As to that, as soon as it can be arranged…'

Mr der Huizma's manner was casual. 'I'm going over to England next week, I could give her a lift back here.'

'You would do that? It would not inconvenience you?'

'Not in the least. Would you let her know? I shall be in England on Saturday and will call at her home early on Sunday morning. We should be back here late on Sunday evening.'

He went home then, to make arrangements for the journey, and after due thought telephoned Mr Gillard.

'It is so fortunate,' he pointed out in his placid voice, 'that I shall be in England next week. I can collect the brooch and Daisy at the same time, provided you have no objection to her leaving early on the Sunday morning. I must be back for a Monday morning clinic.'

'I'm sure Daisy will be glad of a lift,' said Mr Gillard, 'and I'm grateful. I wasn't too happy about her taking that valuable brooch. I'll let her know and she will be ready—eight o'clock and many thanks.'

Daisy's eyes sparkled when she was told. Kindly Fate was giving her a treat. Mr der Huizma loomed large in her mind, but she didn't allow herself to think too much about him. He was the nicest man she had ever met, and she liked him, but he was going to marry Helene and that fact prevented her from allowing her thoughts to wonder about him. To see him again would be delightful, though. Probably he wouldn't speak more than half a dozen words to her, but they would be together for several hours.

She packed her case, rubbed a face cream guaranteed to bring beauty to the dullest visage into her cheeks, and washed her abundant hair. The cream made no difference at all, but she felt better for it and on the strength of its supposed magic qualities bought a new lipstick.

She was to stay with Heer Friske for as long as either she or he wished. Two or three months, she supposed, perhaps longer. Of course there was always the possibility that his wife might not like her, or that she wouldn't pull her weight in the shop. She hoped that would not happen; there was so much to see and learn.

Daisy wrinkled her small nose with pleasure—all those marvellous museums, and those narrow streets lined by antiques shops to explore, as well as getting familiar with the contents of Heer Friske's shop.

She was up early on Sunday morning, eating a hasty breakfast, wearing the new jacket and skirt, pale with excitement, listening to last-minute instructions from her father and quiet sensible comments from her mother.

When Mr der Huizma arrived she hardly spoke beyond replying to his pleasant greeting. He had a cup of coffee, examined the brooch and stowed it away in a pocket, complimenting her on the work she had done on it, then professed himself ready to leave. So she bade her mother and father goodbye and got into the car beside him. Now that the moment of departure had actually come she had the sudden urge to get out of the car again; to stay at home, return to the security and quiet of her life there. Even if she had voiced her wish she would have had no chance to carry it out, for Mr der Huizma drove away without loss of time so that she had only a moment in which to wave goodbye.

'Comfortable?' His voice was calmly reassuring and she relaxed.

'Yes, thank you. It is kind of you to give me a lift…'

'Well, I thought it a good idea to get you and the brooch at the same time, since I was in England. You're happy at the idea of working for Heer Friske?'

'Yes. I liked him; I don't know his wife, though.'

'I'm sure you will be happy with them. You will be kept quite busy, I dare say. His shop is popular with tourists who are looking for genuine antiques; he refuses to sell anything else.'

After that they lapsed into silence—which she had expected anyway. They stopped for coffee mid-morning, and were nearing Harwich before he stopped again for lunch.

'Aren't we a bit early for the ferry?' asked Daisy.

'We're crossing on the new fast ferry—three and a half hours—saves a good deal of time. A catamaran. I came over on it. You'll find it very comfortable.'

When she saw it, Daisy didn't think it looked very

safe. But once on board she changed her mind about that. It was warm and comfortable, and there were easy chairs and plenty of space. It seemed a long time since she had got up that morning; she curled up in a chair and went to sleep.

As a travelling companion she was ideal, decided Mr der Huizma.

She woke instantly at his touch when they docked, her hair slightly tousled, her face shiny with sleep, and she skipped away to tidy herself, to return in good time, once more immaculate, to get into the car again and sit quietly while he drove through the town and onto the motorway.

It was early evening by now, and den Haag, looming ahead of them, looked inviting in the dusk. Daisy was surprised when Mr der Huizma turned off the main road.

'We will have a meal,' he told her. 'You will probably be too tired to eat once we get to Heer Friske. There's a quiet restaurant here, where we can get a meal.'

Daisy was hungry, and did justice to the grilled sole and the massive pudding which followed it—besides, it meant that she could be with him for just a little longer. But they didn't linger over the meal; she sensed that he wished to get home as soon as possible. They drove on presently, and it was with regret that she saw Heer Friske's shop at last. This is the end, she thought.

CHAPTER FIVE

MR DER HUIZMA told Daisy to stay where she was, then got out of the car and rang the bell beside the small door next to the shop. Which gave her ample time in which to wish that she had never come, that she was home again—and then, at the sight of Mr der Huizma's large person standing there, to feel a wave of pleasure at the sight of him.

The door was opened and Heer Friske stood there, smiling. Mr der Huizma came back to the car and opened her door, and got her case from the boot. Her moment of panic was over. She got out and greeted Heer Friske, and was borne indoors and up the stairs to where he and his wife lived, with Mr der Huizma following with her case.

The room they entered was cosy, lived in and warm, and Mevrouw Friske was just as cosy. She made Daisy welcome, and offered coffee. Mr der Huizma refused, with his beautiful manners, and after a few minutes' talk made his farewells. With her hand in his, Daisy thanked him for her lift.

'It was a very pleasant journey,' she told him, aware that she sounded stiff and reserved. 'It was so kind of you to bring me here.'

He stared down at her, not smiling. 'But I wanted the brooch,' he reminded her, 'and since the car was empty it made sense to bring you with me.'

He was still holding her hand. 'I hope that you will be very happy while you are in Amsterdam. Please give my regards to your mother and father when you write. Don't worry about phoning them this evening. I'll do that when I get home.'

He went away then, and Mevrouw Friske bustled her up another flight of stairs to a pretty little room at the front of the house. It was simply furnished but comfortable, with a patchwork quilt on the bed and thick curtains to keep out the winter's cold. There was a shower across the landing, Mevrouw Friske told her, and added anxiously that she hoped Daisy didn't mind being on her own on the top floor. She waited while Daisy took off her coat, and then went back to the living room with her where Heer Friske was waiting.

She was to start work on Tuesday morning; breakfast was at half past seven, the shop opened at half past eight and stayed open until six o'clock—although if there was a customer in the shop it remained open until he or she had gone. Lunch-hour was brief, but there would be a substantial evening meal once the shop had closed. Tomorrow, being Monday, he pointed out, the shop would be closed. 'Which will give you time to settle in,' said Heer

Friske in his correct English. 'And now you will be tired. Coffee and a biscuit with cheese, and you will wish to go to your bed.'

So Daisy spent a short while giving him news of her father and mother and the shop, while Mevrouw Friske sat and knitted, only half understanding but ready with a smile or a motherly word or two, and presently she bade the nice old couple goodnight and went up the steep little staircase to her bed.

And later, tucked up cosily under the quilt, she thought about Mr der Huizma. He would be with Helene, she supposed, and the brooch would be sparkling on Helene's too thin bosom. No doubt they would discuss the date for their wedding. It would be a grand affair; she felt sure that Helene had any number of friends and family. About Mr der Huizma she wasn't so sure; he had barely mentioned his family, never discussed anything to do with his private life, in fact. Perhaps he wasn't close to his family…

In this she was mistaken. He was even at that moment sitting at his ease, with Bouncer lying on his feet, in a great chair on one side of a vast fireplace in a large and elegant room in a house in the country close to Hilversum. It was a square, solid house, with green shutters at its many windows and a vast door reached by double steps, and it stood in large well-kept grounds. The other occupant of the room sat on the other side of the cheerful fire, placidly knitting. A small, rather plump lady, with an elegant hairstyle, no looks to speak of but dressed with great good taste.

She nodded to the elderly woman who had brought in the coffee tray and observed, 'Well, Jules, now that you are here, you must tell me about your trip to England. Your phone call was brief…'

'Dearest, all my phone calls are brief, otherwise I'd never get through my days. I should be home now, catching up on tomorrow's case-sheets, but it seems some time since we saw each other…'

'A month ago,' said his mother, rather tartly. 'You had intended to come a week ago, but Helene had arranged something.'

'Yes. I'm sorry about that. She will be going to California shortly; I'll make it up to you then.'

His mother smiled. 'Jules, dear, it is unkind of me to grumble—I know what a busy life you lead. Tell me, did you have a good journey? You went rather suddenly.'

He began to tell her then. 'The brooch is very beautiful; I must let you see it. And since I was going to fetch it, it seemed sense to bring Daisy back with me.'

'Daisy?'

'I must explain about her…' Which he did, at some length. 'I think you would like her.'

'Is she pretty?'

'No, but she has lovely eyes, a great deal of brown hair and a pretty voice.'

His mother kept her eyes on her knitting. 'She sounds a very nice girl. Quite clever at her work too, I expect.'

'Yes, she is.'

She peeped at her son and saw his smile. 'How did you meet?'

He told her that too. 'And we met again by accident out walking. She doesn't mind the wind and the rain.'

'Then she should like Holland!' said his mother, and they both laughed.

His mother asked presently, 'You will be seeing Helene as soon as possible, of course? I am sure she will be delighted with the brooch—or do you intend giving it to her on your marriage?'

'I think that for the moment I will keep it safe. Helene hasn't decided on a date yet.'

His mother murmured something vague in reply and hoped secretly that Helene would never decide. She had accepted her as a future daughter-in-law because she was devoted to Jules and wanted him to be happy, but she had never liked her—although she had to admit that she was beautiful and, when she wished, charming. She hadn't wasted much charm on her future mother-in-law, though, and barely suppressed her boredom when she visited with Jules, making it plain that she found the house old-fashioned. But she had been careful to do this when Jules hadn't been there. She thought sadly that Helene would do nothing to encourage Jules in his work, nor would she put up with the continuous interruptions which were all part and parcel of his life.

He got up to go then, with a promise that he would visit her again as soon as he could.

'Do, Jules. If Helene is away and you are free on a Sunday we could spend the day together.'

He went back home then, with Bouncer sitting beside him, and found himself wishing that it was Daisy sitting there.

When Daisy went down to breakfast the following morning she was told to go and enjoy herself. 'Time enough to start work tomorrow,' said Heer Friske. 'It is your chance to buy stamps and postcards, and see where the nearest shops are.'

So Daisy made her bed, tidied her room, helped Mevrouw Friske with the washing up and then took herself off to explore. She remembered from her first visit where the nearest shops were. There were shops all round Heer Friske's; shops given over to antiques, like his, shops selling the kind of thing tourists wanted to buy—pictures, Delft china, modern silver—but the kind of shops she sought were at the end of the street some five minutes' walk away. A post office, a stationer's, a shabby little shop selling wool and haberdashery and cheap souvenirs, a bakery and a small supermarket.

Quite sufficient for her needs, she decided. There would be little chance to go to the Kalverstraat or Leidestraat and look in the elegant shop windows there, but since she had very little money she didn't suppose that would matter. She bought stamps, postcards and an English newspaper, and went back to the shop. It was almost noon, and there was a delicious smell coming from the kitchen. She took her things to her room and offered to set the table for lunch. Presently Heer Friske came in and they sat down to thick pea soup, full of tiny pieces of sausage and pork, accompanied by thick slices of bread.

'My wife makes the best *echte* soup in Amsterdam,' observed Heer Friske, offering second helpings.

The shop opened the next day at eight-thirty, but there were only a few customers; Daisy looked and listened and stored away any amount of useful information. An old lady came in with a Delft plate. It was in mint condition and Heer Friske asked Daisy what she thought its value might be. She examined it carefully, looking for damage and repairs and finding neither, and named a sum, thankful for hours she had spent poring over *Miller's Antiques* and the close attention she had always paid at auction sales.

Heer Friske looked pleased. 'A fair estimate,' he told her. 'When the shop is closed this evening we will look at what Delftware I have and you will learn more…'

So that evening, after a substantial meal of pork chops, red cabbage and boiled potatoes, followed by something Mevrouw Friske called 'pudding' but which Daisy rechristened custard, they went back downstairs and inspected the Delft china. There wasn't a great deal of it, but what there was was genuine and valuable. Daisy went to bed a good deal wiser about it, and lay in bed going over everything that Heer Friske had told her. She could see that there was a great deal that she must learn—but that was why she had come, wasn't it?

Almost asleep, she amended that. She had come not only to increase her knowledge of antiques but so that she might have a chance of seeing Mr der Huizma once in a while. Amsterdam wasn't such a very large city, and the hospital wasn't far from the shop…

The week went quickly, and if the long hours in the shop were tiring, she knew that she was learning all the time. She had waited upon one or two customers—Americans, glad to find someone who spoke English and was willing to chat for a little while while they looked through the silver intent on taking back something from Holland. They were only small sales, but Daisy was delighted; she had broken the ice and felt that she was worth her small salary.

She had been told that she was to come and go as she wished on Sunday. The Friskes seldom went out, but family and friends visited them, and occasionally they spent the day with Mevrouw Friske's sister. Daisy was given a key and told to get herself a meal if she felt inclined and there was no one home.

On that first Sunday she didn't venture far. After breakfast she walked to the Oude Kerk and went back for the midday meal with the Friskes. She went out again in the afternoon, and took a tour of the canals in one of the glass-topped boats, and afterwards found a small café where she had tea and a cream cake of gigantic proportions. And all the while she kept an eye open for Mr der Huizma…

She spent the evening watching Dutch television with the Friskes and went to bed early. Next week she would venture further afield. Perhaps take a train or a bus to Delft or den Haag. There were endless possibilities, she told herself.

She was getting into the swing of things now, and the next week went quickly. She was making herself useful in the shop, and when there were no customers she listened to Heer Friske explaining the history of marquetry and examining one or two fine specimens which were in the shop. And when Saturday came she made careful plans for Sunday. She would take a bus to Vollendam, a favourite venue for tourists, and a kind of showplace of Holland as it had been. The buses went from Central Station and she knew where that was. She would have a snack lunch there and come back in the afternoon, and then if there were still some hours to spare, she would go and look at the shops in Leidesgracht and Vijselstraat.

The last customer went and she started to take the more valuable antiques out of the window while Heer Friske locked up the takings and the valuable silver. When the phone rang he called her over. 'For you, Daisy.'

She picked up the phone quickly; her mother had telephoned during the week, and there was no reason for her to ring again unless there was something wrong. She said, 'Hullo,' in a worried voice, and then 'hullo' again, in a quite different voice, when she heard who it was.

'Jules der Huizma. I have a free day tomorrow; do you care to have a drive with me so that I can show you something of Holland?'

'Oh, yes, please. I'd love to do that.' Daisy was breathless with delight.

'Good. I'll pick you up at ten o'clock.'

'I'll be ready.' And then, as a thought struck her, she said, 'But don't you want to spend it with Helene? Is she coming too? She might not like it…'

He sounded faintly amused. 'Helene is in California, but I am quite sure that she would have no objection to me taking you on a sightseeing trip.'

'Oh, well. If you are sure…'

'Quite sure,' said Mr der Huizma. He put the phone down and addressed Bouncer. 'We are going to have a day out, Bouncer, and we are going to enjoy every minute of it.'

He had spent two weeks thinking about Daisy. Sooner or later she would go back home and he need never see her again—indeed he *must* never see her again. He must forget her, or do his best to do so; she must never intrude into the future. A future with Helene as his wife. But he was not yet married.

Daisy was up early on Sunday morning, taking pains with her face and her hair, glad that it was a dry day, even if chilly, so that she could wear the coat and skirt. Sensible shoes, she decided, in case they did some walking, and the silk scarf her mother had given her to tie over her hair. There was always a wind in Holland, or so it seemed to her. She ate her breakfast under the Friskes' kindly eyes and went pink with excitement when the doorbell rang.

Mr der Huizma came upstairs and spent ten

minutes talking to the Friskes before asking her if she was ready, then whisking her down to the car and popping her into it. Bouncer was already there, pleased to see her, and he sat squashed between her and his master's bulk.

'He can sit in the back if you prefer?'

Daisy patted the silky head. 'He would be lonely; besides, I like him. I wish we had a dog at home, but he would be needing walks and company…'

She looked around her as he drove through the quiet streets away from the centre of the city. 'Where are we going?'

'To the coast first. Zandvoort. We'll have coffee there. Tell me, Daisy, are you happy with Heer Friske?'

'Oh, yes. They are both so kind to me, and the shop's quite busy—he's well known, isn't he? And I'm learning a lot—marquetry and Beidermeyer and I didn't know that Holland had such an enormous variety of Delft blue. Heer Friske has an almost perfect eighteenth-century ewer, and some beautiful tiles. Father hasn't any of those. Perhaps Heer Friske will let him have some; I could take them back when I go.'

Mr der Huizma glanced at her. 'You are already thinking of returning to England?'

'Heavens, no. I'd like to stay for a couple of months, if Heer Friske will have me. There's so much that I don't know.' She turned a beaming smile on him. 'Isn't it lucky that it isn't raining? Are we going to take Bouncer for a run?'

'Of course, but coffee first.'

Daisy, quite at her ease now, said, 'I have a door key; the Friskes are going to visit friends and my dinner is all ready for me to warm up. Mevrouw Friske is so kind, and we get on so well. It's a bit difficult sometimes, when we don't quite understand each other, but I'm learning fast—just useful words. Dutch is a frightful language, isn't it?'

'So I have been told, but since it is my mother tongue I don't feel qualified to comment.'

Daisy had gone bright pink. 'I'm sorry, that was rude of me—although I didn't mean it to be.'

'I do know that, Daisy, and surely we are sufficiently acquainted by now to be at ease with each other?'

'Well, I suppose we are acquainted, but it's not like being friends.' She frowned. 'It's difficult to explain, but you're you and I'm me…'

He didn't pretend not to understand her. 'Nevertheless, I believe that we are friends, Daisy.'

They were travelling along a country road and he pulled in onto the grass verge. He offered a large hand. 'Friends, Daisy?'

She shook the hand and beamed at him. 'Oh, yes, please.'

'And now that is settled once and for all, you might call me Jules?'

'All right, I will,' she went on. 'You know, I have always felt that we were friends, only I didn't think you had thought about it.'

Mr der Huizma reflected that he had thought about it a great deal during the last two weeks or so, but he didn't say so. He said briskly, 'We're going to Leiden now. I was a student at the medical school there; it's a charming little town. We won't stop, though, since we shall lunch in Delft.'

All the same he did stop obligingly so that she might see the Burcht, a twelfth-century mound with a fortress on the top, right in the middle of the town, and he stopped again so that she might have a glimpse of the Rapenburg Canal and the university and the museum.

'Were you happy there?' asked Daisy.

'Yes. I go back from time to time; it's full of pleasant memories.'

He drove on to Delft then, parking near the Grote Markt and taking her to a small restaurant where she could see both the town hall and the Nieuwe Kerk standing facing each other across the market square.

He didn't ask her what she would like to eat. 'This is a typical Dutch meal,' he told her. 'I hope you're hungry.'

She was, which was a good thing, for presently a

waitress brought two large plates covered by vast pancakes dotted with tiny bits of crisp bacon. She also brought a big pot of dark syrup.

Mr der Huizma ladled the syrup onto the pancakes. 'It looks crazy but it tastes delicious,' he told her. And it was.

Daisy ate all of it with an enjoyment which brought a gleam of pleasure into Mr der Huizma's eyes. They drank a pot of coffee between them before he took her across to the Nieuwe Kerk. 'William of Orange is buried here, as well as other members of the royal family. You must come again and spend some time here; it's a delightful little town and very Dutch. And now is the time of year to see it, before the tourists come.'

They got back into the car and he told her, 'We're going to drive across to Hilversum. We'll pass Alphen aan de Rijn on the way—there's a bird sanctuary there—and we will pass Gouda too—that's for another time—there are some lakes close by—Reeuwijk Meer—you'll get a glimpse of them.'

She supposed after that they would return to Amsterdam. It was almost four o'clock now, and the afternoon had grown grey and chilly, but presently they joined a main road and she saw the signpost to Hilversum.'

'You're going the wrong way,' said Daisy. 'Amsterdam was that road on the left.'

'We must have tea first.' He didn't enlarge on that, and she presumed that there was a café or tea room he particularly wanted to go to. The country was pretty, even on this rather bleak day. There were small woods and narrow roads, and here and there a glimpse of a large house behind the trees. The trees and bushes soon thinned out along the side of the road, and she had a fine view of a large square house standing well back from the road, backed by trees. It was white with green shutters, and its many windows climbed up to a steep roof.

'Oh, look,' said Daisy, 'what a lovely house. It looks as though it's been there for ever, and it looks cosy although it's rather large. And look, the windows are lighted. I expect it houses a family with children and dogs and cats.'

Mr der Huizma swept the car between tall gateposts. 'Well, not at present,' he observed, 'but possibly one day. And it is a cosy house; I was born in it.'

Daisy turned to look at him. 'But you have a lovely house in Amsterdam.'

'This is the family home. My mother lives here; we are going to have tea with her.'

'But she doesn't know me.'

'Well, no. She hasn't met you yet, has she?'

He stopped the car before the house, and got out and opened the door for her.

'I'm not sure,' began Daisy doubtfully.

He said bracingly. 'Come, come, where is your British phlegm? And I'm sure you would like a cup of tea.'

He greeted the elderly woman who opened the door as they went up the steps, and then said, 'This is Katje, our housekeeper. She doesn't speak English but understands a few words.' So Daisy shook hands and smiled, and was smiled at in return. 'Let her have your jacket; she will show you where the cloak-room is.'

Daisy followed Katje to the back of the square hall and was ushered into a small room equipped, as far as she could see, with everything a woman might need. Having tidied her hair and powdered her nose she went back into the hall to find Jules standing there, where she had left him.

He opened an arched double door, and with a hand on her shoulder walked her into the room beyond. His mother was sitting in her usual chair by the fire, and she got up as they went in.

'Jules, how nice to see you—and so punctual too.' She offered a cheek for his kiss and turned to Daisy, smiling.

'Mother, this is Daisy Gillard, over here to learn something of our antiques.' His mother, already aware of that, smiled and offered a hand. 'My mother,' said Mr der Huizma, and watched them shake hands, still smiling, and then he smiled himself, because it was all right; they liked each other…

Tea, to Daisy's relief, wasn't just a cup of weak tea and a tiny biscuit. The tea was a fragrant Assam and there were tiny sandwiches as well as scones and a fruitcake. Sitting there by the fire, listening to her hostess's quiet voice going from one unalarming topic to another, was a delight. Beyond a few casual questions about herself, Mevrouw der Huizma made no attempt to cross-examine her. The talk was desultory and unforced; it was as if the three of them had known each other all their lives. Well, of course Jules and his mother had, hadn't they? reflected Daisy, biting into a second slice of cake, but somehow she seemed to be included in the family.

But she couldn't presume on such kindness; when the great *stoel* clock struck six she suggested that she should go back to Amsterdam. 'The Friskes expect me back in the evening,' she pointed out, which wasn't quite true but it sounded all right. So presently she bade Mevrouw der Huizma goodbye, thanked her for her tea, and got back into the car with Jules and Bouncer.

And if she was secretly disappointed that he hadn't urged her to stay longer, she squashed the thought at once as being ungrateful. He had, after all, spent the whole day driving around Holland with her, when he might have spent it doing something more exciting.

To her relief there were lights from the Friskes' upstairs windows, so that her fib appeared justified. As Mr der Huizma stopped before their door she began the little speech she had thought about on their way, but she didn't get far with it. He interrupted her with, 'Daisy, spare me the thanks I'm sure you have been rehearsing. I have enjoyed my day with you; you're a good companion, you know. You don't talk unless you have something to say, and then it's good sense, and you're blessedly silent…'

Daisy said, 'Oh, am I?' in a surprised voice, not sure if she liked the bit about her being silent; had she talked too much? She was aware that, whereas she was usually reserved with people, with Jules she felt so much at ease that she might have let her tongue run away with her.

He got out and opened her door and they crossed the cobbles to the door.

'If I am free next Sunday we will drive up to the Frisian lakes and take a look at Leeuwarden.'

He took the key from her hand and opened the door, then stood looking down at her, and she smiled at him, delighted that she would see him again. Despite himself he kissed her upturned face, then gave her a gentle shove through the door and closed it before she had the chance to say goodnight. Which was just as well for she was too astonished to speak.

She made her way upstairs to the Friskes' sitting room in a bemused manner, answered their questions as to how she had spent her day and presently sat down to *echte* soup and smoked sausage and *zuurkoel*. And all the while she was thinking about his kiss. Of course everyone kissed these days, she told herself sensibly, but it hadn't been a social kiss, had it? It had been warm and lingering; there had been nothing social about it. She decided to forget it.

Easier said than done, she discovered, but as the next Sunday approached she warned herself sternly to let Jules see that it had made no impression upon her, that it had been something easily forgotten. Moreover, she decided that if he should suggest any more outings she would refuse. It was no good saying that she was spending the day with friends, for she had none as yet. She could have a heavy cold—so much more plausible than a headache…unless it was a migraine. But perhaps he wouldn't ask her out again; Helene would be coming back from California and he would spend his spare time with her. It was quite natural, Daisy told herself, that a man should spend his free time with a companion if his fiancée wasn't there with him. Which was where she ought to be, thought Daisy.

She had expected to feel awkward when he called

for her on Sunday, but his quiet friendliness dispelled that at once.

It was a damp grey day, with the threat of rain, but the car was warm and comfortable and Bouncer was glad to see her again.

'We shall go to Alkmaar, and then on to the Afsluitdijk to Friesland,' he told her, 'and we shall come back for part of the way through the reclaimed land from the Ijsselmeer. The reclaiming is still going on, and the country isn't very interesting, but there are any number of farms there and they're prosperous.'

After that he didn't say much, only asking from time to time if she had enjoyed her week. She answered him briefly, mindful of his remarks about being silent, and asked instead if he had had an interesting week.

It struck him that Helene had never asked him that, and he began to tell her a little of his work. Daisy asked questions: How many children were in his wards? Did he operate? Were the children happy in hospital? What happened when they were discharged home? And did he like the babies or the toddlers best?

And he answered her questions in detail, realising what a pleasure it was to talk about his work to someone who was really interested and not just polite. Of course he talked to his mother, but he saw her infrequently and there was always family news to discuss so that he seldom did more than touch lightly on his work, but now, with Daisy all ears beside him, listening eagerly to his replies, he told her all that she wanted to know and found himself enjoying talking of it.

In Alkmaar they stopped for coffee and a brisk walk through the little town as far as the cheese market and the Weigh House with its carillon, before driving over the Afsluitdijk into Friesland. He drove through Harlingen and Franeker and on to Leeuwarden, where they had lunch at a hotel and another quick walk for Bouncer's benefit and for a view of the statue of the cow—the sign of Friesland's prosperity.

And then it was on again to Sneek, and the lakes, and on to Meppel and so to Lelystad, one of the small towns on the reclaimed land, and thence to Naarden and Hilversum.

'Mother is expecting us for tea,' said Mr der Huizma, turning in between the pillars.

And it was all just as delightful as the previous Sunday had been, sitting in the grand room, with Bouncer close to his master, scoffing the odd pieces of cake or biscuit, and a large ginger cat sitting beside Mevrouw der Huizma in her chair, so that the room didn't seem grand at all, just a room where people were happy and content. Daisy, unable to put it into coherent thought, felt a quiet happiness. Heart's ease, she thought, that's what I'm feeling.

She took care not to outstay her welcome. Mevrouw der Huizma kissed her goodbye. 'I'm sure we shall see each other again,' she observed—something which Daisy secretly hoped for. But Jules said nothing about a further meeting when they reached Heer Friske's house. Nor did he kiss her, but bade her goodbye in a cheerful brisk manner and told her not to work too hard.

So I'm not going to see him again, Daisy told herself, getting ready for bed. Helene would be coming back. He would give her the diamond brooch and they would marry. She was almost asleep before she voiced her thoughts. 'But they won't live happily ever after!'

The shop was unusually busy the following week, and Daisy, having mastered some essential Dutch, found herself fully occupied. The tourists were beginning to drift in, and each evening Heer Friske taught her all he knew about marquetry and Dutch porcelain.

When the weekend came, Daisy took herself off to various small side-streets lined by antique dealers' shops, and studied their windows before having an early lunch in a café and spending the afternoon in the Rijksmuseum. She had a cup of tea there, and stayed until it closed. As she left its entrance she saw Mr der Huizma in his car. Helene was sitting beside him, but Bouncer was on the back seat. He didn't see her; indeed, both of them were looking ahead, not speaking…

So Helene was back. At the back of her mind Daisy had had the vague hope that she might like California so much that she had decided to stay there. So now I can stop being silly, Daisy told herself, walking briskly back for her supper. It was nice knowing him, but now I can forget him.

Which should have been easy, but Fate sometimes disregards the best of intentions.

It was on a morning towards the end of the next week that Daisy, rubbing up some silver candlesticks while Heer Friske was talking a customer into buying some Dutch tiles, was distracted by a great deal of noise in the street outside. Heer Friske was occupied, so she put down her cloth and went out of the shop to take a look.

A car had stopped close by, and an elderly woman was sitting on the cobbles clutching a large black cat while the driver stooped over her. He looked up as Daisy reached them.

'Do you speak English? I wasn't driving fast but the cat ran across the street and she came after it.'

'I'm English,' said Daisy, and mustered a few Dutch words. The woman shook her head. No, she wasn't hurt, nothing was broken; she was just sore.

Daisy put two and two together, patted her shoulder reassuringly, stroked the cat and said, 'Look, I think you'd better take her to hospital. It's not far. Wait a minute while I speak to Heer Friske.'

The car driver mopped a worried brow. 'Will you come? I'm very grateful—I'll pay.'

Heer Friske, having sold his tiles, came hurrying out on Daisy's heels, explained to the woman, helped the driver get her into the car, still holding the cat, and told Daisy to go with them. He turned to the man. 'And bring her back when everything is settled.'

So Daisy got into the car beside the driver and steered him through the streets to the hospital. Once there, she went into Casualty and found the sister. She remembered her, so that explaining what had happened wasn't difficult. The woman was led away and Daisy, having been handed the cat, wondered what to do next. The driver was talking to the receptionist and they were soon joined by a large police officer. She held the cat securely and joined them.

'Will someone tell the patient that I'll take the cat back to her home? Only I must know her address and have a key to get in.' She turned to Sister. 'Could you explain that I'm at Heer Friske's and that I'm quite honest. I'll get a taxi—I can't wait any longer.' She looked at the driver and the officer, deep in talk. A few minutes later she had the key and the address and was on her way to the hospital entrance. And a few yards from it she met Mr der Huizma, also on his way out.

CHAPTER SIX

THERE was no avoiding Jules, nor, apparently, had he any intention of letting her try to do so.

'Daisy...' He took in the cat tucked under her arm with a quick glance. 'You're leaving the hospital? I'll drive you back.'

Anyone else would have bombarded her with questions, thought Daisy, but not Jules. She took a firmer grip on the cat, gave a brief resumé of events and waited to see what he would say.

'We will take the cat back home,' said Mr der Huizma without hesitation, 'warn a neighbour, if possible, and return you to Heer Friske's shop. He must be worried. This lady is in Casualty? Is she injured?'

And when Daisy said that she didn't know he said, 'Well, never mind that now; I can find out easily enough. Just leave it to me.'

He swept her out to the car, glanced at the address Sister had written down for Daisy, and drove off. It was a small house in a row of small houses, very neat, with gleaming windows and spotless curtains, and inside the whole place shone with polish. The furniture was old, but cared for, and behind the tiny kitchen there was a garden, very small and as neat as the house. The cat went at once to a chair in the corner of the living room, curled up and prepared to sleep, quite untroubled by the goings-on around it. Daisy found a saucer, filled it with cat food and put it on the kitchen floor, and Mr der Huizma went next door to talk to a neighbour.

He came back presently. 'We are to leave the kitchen window open so that the cat can get in and out; the neighbour will feed him if necessary.'

'The key?' asked Daisy.

He took his phone from his pocket and she waited patiently while he talked and listened and talked again. 'The patient is to come home presently. She isn't seriously hurt—bruises and a small cut on her leg. Let me have the key and I will see that she gets it. I shall be going back to the hospital.'

Something which hadn't been his intention but he was a kind man. He added, 'Come along, I'll drive you back to Heer Friske.'

Daisy had barely spoken; delight at seeing him again had rendered her speechless. He had taken command of the situation and she had been willing to do as she was told. Now she said, 'You've been very kind, but I can walk back; it's not far…'

He had gone to open the little window in the kitchen. 'I shall be going past the shop,' was all he said.

He left her there presently, bidding her a brisk goodbye and driving away before she could utter thanks. Back to the hospital which he had so recently left for a few hours before he saw his private patients in the evening. He reflected ruefully that on almost all of the occasions when he and Daisy had met she had disrupted his plans. And now she had popped up again to disturb him. They had exchanged barely a dozen words, and yet he had enjoyed every minute of her silent company. He frowned, remembering that he had resolved not to see her again. Her small, quiet person had begun to fill his thoughts, something which had to be stopped.

He went into the hospital and sought out the sister in Casualty, who told him that the woman was ready to be discharged and then asked him if Helene was back from California. She was a long-standing friend and colleague, anxious to see him happily married. She didn't like Helene, whom she had met at various hospital functions, but thought she seemed entirely suitable. She was surprised to see the look on Mr der Huizma's handsome face when he told her that she had recently returned home. Surely a man shouldn't look like that when speaking of the woman he was to marry?

She prudently said nothing more, but went to fetch the cat's owner.

Mr der Huizma drove her home, gave her back

her key and listened with pleasure to her gratitude towards Daisy. 'Such a kind young lady. Came to help me at once, and understood how I felt about my cat. And her a foreigner too.'

The temptation to stop at Heer Friske's shop on the way home was great, but he resisted it. Meeting Daisy had been unavoidable, but to seek her out deliberately was quite another thing.

He went home, and later to his consulting rooms, and when he finally got back to eat a late dinner there was a message from Helene. She would expect to hear from him in the morning.

Mr der Huizma looked through his diary. He had a busy few days ahead of him; there would be very little time to see Helene and certainly no chance to take her out to dinner or the theatre, which he thought she would expect. He made a note to have flowers sent to her home and settled down at his desk to continue writing an article on infant malnutrition. He had been asked if he would go to the famine areas in Africa and advise on the feeding of the starving babies and children there, and he had decided to go. It was something dear to his heart, and he had contrived to arrange his work so that he could go for a month. He paused in his writing and sighed; Helene wasn't going to like his decision. It was a pity he hadn't been able to arrange it while she was in California…

* * *

On the following Monday morning Daisy called on the woman with the cat. She had been to the post office, bought herself a newspaper, some toothpaste and a bottle of shampoo and, as an afterthought, a tin of cat food. The woman came to the door when she knocked; she recognised her and asked her in.

Daisy, at a loss for words, held out the cat food, and right on cue the cat came into the room and walked over to her, weaving round her feet. The woman beamed, keeping up a flow of talk, none of which Daisy understood. When the woman paused for breath Daisy ventured, 'Better?' and, since it was a word very similar to its Dutch counterpart, the woman nodded and smiled, waved Daisy to a chair and went out of the room to return with a letter in her hand. She gave it to Daisy and pointed and nodded so Daisy took it out of its envelope. It was in English, and was from the man who had knocked the woman down. There was money inside too. She read the letter and then, dredging up the words she knew, explained that the money was compensation for the accident. Her accent was shocking, but with a good deal of hand-waving and nodding she made her companion understand.

She gave the letter and the money back, and when she would have got up was waved back to her seat. 'Coffee?' said her hostess, and since Daisy had an hour to spare, and the cat had scrambled onto her lap, she stayed in the neat little room, carrying on what passed for conversation with the woman.

When she got up to go she realised that she had enjoyed herself, and learnt quite a few more Dutch words. Never mind the grammar, she decided. Knowing what everything was called in Dutch was the priority. Never mind the accent either; Heer Friske would put her right with that. She went back to the shop feeling that perhaps she was making a little niche for herself; perhaps she would meet people and make friends.

Mr der Huizma, preparing for his journey, working early and late and making up in part for his forthcoming absence, had told Helene of his intention.

She had phoned him and told him that he could take her out to dinner. 'There's that new restaurant in the Leidesgracht,' she had said. 'We'll go there; you'll have to book a table…'

She had rung off before he could speak.

The dinner hadn't been a success. They had almost finished their meal before she'd asked him if he had been busy. 'Your boring job,' she'd said, laughing at him across the table. 'We must go out more…'

'I'm going away,' he had told her quietly, and had explained why he was going.

'But it will be ghastly,' she'd exclaimed. 'You'll

pick up one of those horrible diseases. There are dozens of young doctors willing to go, I'm sure. Really, Jules, I can't allow you to do it.'

His eyes had been cold. 'I'm afraid there is no question of your allowing me to do anything, Helene. This is my work and I intend to do it. I thought you might have understood…'

She had been pale with annoyance. 'Understood? I'm not some GP's wife, meekly accepting a dreary life of interrupted nights and uneaten meals. Life's meant to be enjoyed and I intend to enjoy it.'

He had stayed silent for a moment, and then said quietly, 'If that is how you feel, Helene, perhaps we should reconsider…'

She had seen that she had gone too far. 'Jules, I'm sorry. Of course you must do what you think right. Only you frightened me for a moment…' She'd smiled at him, the picture of contrition. 'Forgive me?'

'Of course, but I do not intend to change my mind, Helene.'

She had said quickly, 'No, no, of course not. You must tell me about it—how long will you be gone?'

She had infused interest into her voice. For a few moments she had been afraid that she would lose him; as a husband he was all, or almost all, that a woman could wish for.

She had kissed him warmly when they parted, but

for Jules it could have been as unimportant as something half felt and brushed away with no further thought. He was aware now that Helene didn't love him, never had, perhaps, but knew he represented everything that she wanted from life. She had no intention of releasing him from their engagement, and for his part would have been content with that—until he had met Daisy, whom he must forget, and who would go back to England and eventually marry some man or stay single. She had never been more than friendly, he reflected ruefully; it had been his misfortune to fall in love with a girl who didn't care twopence about him.

He was to leave in a week's time, and every minute that he could spare he spent with Helene, trying to rekindle his feelings for her. But she, secure as to her future, brushed aside his suggestions that they should marry.

'For heaven's sake,' she had told him impatiently, 'I'll have years of being a wife, running our home and planning our social life. I mean to have some fun before then.' She'd pouted prettily. 'Jules, if only you would have fun too. You're thirty-five, and as far as I can tell your life's one dreary round of hospitals and patients and giving lectures.'

'But that is my life and I'm happy with it, Helene. You can always change your mind...'

Once again she'd had a moment's uncertainty, but

she was too self-centred to let it worry her. 'Dear Jules, of course I won't change my mind. When you get back we'll fix a date for the wedding.'

He said nothing to his mother when he visited her, but that lady, watching him on one of his rare visits, saw that something wasn't right. She had enquired about Helene, as she always did, and received his vague replies in silence. But when she asked if he had seen Daisy and saw the look on his face she felt troubled. Unless Helene gave him a good reason for doing so Jules would never break their engagement—and Helene wasn't likely to do so. But that, reflected Mevrouw der Huizma silently, is what I hope and pray will happen.

Daisy was up early on the morning Jules was to leave for Africa. She had neither seen nor heard anything of him, which should have made it easy to forget him, only it hadn't. She thought about him a good deal, despite her resolution not to do so, and now, on this bright spring morning, she was in the shop packing up some china a customer was to call for on his way to the airport. Mevrouw Friske was upstairs, getting breakfast, and Heer Friske was still in bed. The street outside was empty save for early tradesmen.

She had her back to the door when the old-fashioned bell tinkled, and she glanced at the clock as she hurried to open it. The customer was early; he would have to wait for a few minutes.

She pulled up the blind as she opened the door, and stood back wordlessly as Mr der Huizma walked in.

'We're not open,' said Daisy, and, as an after thought, 'Good morning.'

He made no reply to either of those remarks. 'I'm going away—for a month, perhaps longer.' His eyes searched her face. 'I didn't want to go without saying goodbye. I'm going to Africa.'

'But you'll be back?' Her heart had sunk into her shoes, but she was glad to hear her voice sounding normal.

'Oh, yes. Will you be gone?'

'I don't know. Perhaps. Why are you going to Africa?' she added. 'It's a long way.'

'I'm going to organise a hospital and feeding centre for the children in a famine area.'

'Yes, of course; they must need someone like you. If I were a nurse I'd have liked to have gone with you.' And when he said nothing she added, 'Helene must be sorry that you're going.'

As indeed she was—but for all the wrong reasons.

He said harshly, 'Helene has a great many interests to keep her happy while I'm away. Will you miss me? Daisy?'

She studied his calm face. 'Yes, of course I shall.

One always misses friends, and we are friends, remember? But I don't see you often—hardly at all, and then it's by accident.' She sighed. 'But, yes, I'll miss you. But I wish you success,' she added, 'and a quick return home.' She put out a hand, suddenly aware that if he stayed much longer she would burst into tears. 'Goodbye.'

He took her hand and held it carefully, as though it might break, then he swept her into his arms and kissed her. It was a kiss not to be easily forgotten. Indeed Daisy hadn't known kisses like that existed outside romantic novels.

'I have to have something,' said Mr der Huizma in a goaded voice, and released her so violently that she nearly fell over.

'Well,' said Daisy, but she spoke to an empty shop. The Rolls was already on its silent way.

It would never do to burst into tears, although she very much wanted to. Instead she sucked in her breath like a hurt child, and finished packing the china. Presently, called to her breakfast by Mevrouw Friske, she went upstairs and drank her coffee. To eat would have choked her; she pleaded a headache which she was sure would soon go, and agreed with Mevrouw Friske that she would make up for her lack of appetite at their midday meal.

Mr der Huizma, handing over the car to Joop, who had accompanied him to Schipol, boarded his plane and allowed his thoughts to dwell on Daisy. She had been pleased to see him, he was sure of that, but she had said nothing which would allow him to hope that she had any warmer feelings for him. And a good thing too, he reminded himself. That she should be made unhappy was something he would not be able to bear. He hadn't intended to kiss her, that had been a mistake, but one which he realised he had been powerless to prevent. He hoped that she would consider it as a farewell kiss and nothing more. He didn't think that she was a girl who had been kissed very often, and she would probably think that it was a normal goodbye. After all they were friends; she had said so.

And now he must forget her, and consider the work ahead of him. He got out his paperwork and began to study it, dismissing Daisy from his mind. He hadn't thought once about Helene. For the moment his personal problems must take second place.

Daisy got through her day somehow. She knew how awful it was to love someone who didn't love you. True, he had kissed her quite savagely, but he hadn't really minded when she had told him that she would probably be gone by the time he returned. If she had been other than a sensible girl, who had learned that she wasn't particularly attractive to men, she might have built her hopes on that kiss. As it was she decided that he had been upset at leaving his home and Helene and had needed to express his feelings.

A sensible conclusion, which didn't prevent herself from crying till she fell asleep that night. It was so awful that she wouldn't see him again—she would be home before he returned, she felt sure—but what was worse was that she had no idea where he had gone, nor would she hear news of him. And how silly of her to fall in love with a man who was on the point of getting married to a very beautiful woman, and who lived in a different world to her own.

Hearts didn't break, Daisy assured herself, and life must go on, and in a little while she would be able to think of him as one thought of a pleasant dream. She would apply herself wholeheartedly to the study of Dutch antiques, strive even harder to acquire some knowledge of the Dutch tongue, and on her free Sundays see as much of the country as she could.

These high-minded resolutions took her through the week following Jules's departure, and she planned a whole day's outing on Sunday. It would involve buses and trains, and she would probably get lost, but it would keep her fully occupied and it would be something to write home about…

There was a letter for her on Saturday morning; a vellum envelope, and addressed in a fine, spidery handwriting. Her heart had leapt at the sight of it and then common sense had taken over. Mr der Huizma had no reason to write to her, and she doubted if expensive notepaper was readily obtained where he was living now. She opened it, and spread out the sheet of fine notepaper it contained. It was from Mevrouw der Huizma. Would she have lunch and spend the afternoon with her on Sunday? Joop would fetch her and bring her back. Perhaps she would phone and let her know.

Daisy read the letter twice, and then sat thinking about it. She would love to go, she liked Mevrouw der Huizma and she wanted to see Jules's home again, but would it be better if she were to refuse? Going to his home would keep alive the memories she was trying so hard to forget. But he wasn't there, she reminded herself…

She went to tell Heer Friske, and then telephoned her acceptance.

Joop came to fetch her soon after eleven o'clock. Daisy had spent some time searching her scanty wardrobe for something suitable for the occasion, but really there wasn't anything there to match the magnificence of his home. It would have to be the jacket and skirt again, and a plain silk blouse. Not that it mattered, reflected Daisy, studying as much as possible of her person in the small looking glass in her room. Jules wasn't there, and even if he was, he wouldn't notice what she was wearing.

Joop, driving an elderly Daimler, greeted her in a fatherly fashion and looked pleased when she got in beside him. He drove well, but at a discreet pace, which gave her time to practise her Dutch on him. He replied in the same language, gently correcting her when her verbs became too tangled. At the house he ushered her out of the car and into the house. Katje took her jacket and led the way to the drawing room.

Mevrouw der Huizma was sitting in her usual chair, Bouncer beside her. She got up to greet Daisy with every sign of pleasure.

'Sit down, Daisy. Katje will bring coffee in a moment. This is kind of you to bear me company. I wondered if you would like to see round the house presently? There are some rather nice pieces, and I know you are interested in antiques. But first let us have coffee and chat. How are you getting on?'

They talked comfortably over coffee, but Jules wasn't mentioned. Daisy, who had been hoping to hear something of him, was disappointed, but perhaps later…

They began a tour of the house presently. 'For there is a lot to see,' explained her hostess. 'The ground floor will take us until lunch time.'

Daisy would have liked to have spent more time

in the drawing room; it held some splendid specimens of marquetry and a collection of porcelain she could have spent hours over, but she followed Mevrouw der Huizma out of the room to linger in the dining room, with its magnificent Regency sideboard and panelled walls hung with family portraits in heavy frames. Daisy, peering up at them, thought that Jules looked very like his ancestors, even though he didn't wear a wig. But she didn't say so as she followed her hostess into a small room with striped wallpaper, comfortable chairs and a round games table under the window. There was nothing modern there, but it would be a delightful room in which to sit and do nothing…

'I sit here a great deal,' said Mevrouw der Huizma, 'sewing and knitting and writing letters. The grandchildren call it Granny's Room.'

'Oh—do you have many? Grandchildren?'

'Five, so far. I have two daughters. I hope for more grandchildren when Jules marries.'

Daisy said steadily, 'I'm sure you must do. Children are such fun, and this house is made for them, isn't it? I mean, it's rather grand and large, but it's home…'

Mevrouw der Huizma gave her a look of deep approval. Here was a girl after her own heart, and, she suspected, Jules's heart too. She sighed and led the way to the library, and the study, and then into the vast conservatory at the back of the house.

Presently, drinking sherry before lunch, once more in the drawing room, she said, 'You must come again, Daisy, and roam around as much as you please. Everything is catalogued, which may help you.'

'I should like that very much, *mevrouw*. But I'm not sure how much longer I shall be at Heer Friske's…'

They lunched in the dining room, sitting together at one end of the long table; melon balls, jellied lobster, salad, and a sponge pudding swimming in sherry and thick cream. Daisy, undeterred by the eyes of Jules's ancestors staring down at her from the walls, enjoyed every morsel.

It was as they sat drinking their coffee in the drawing room that Mevrouw der Huizma observed, 'I was glad to hear from Jules this week. A brief note brought by one of the nurses returning to Holland. He says very little, but I gather that there is a tremendous amount of work to be done there and they need skilled men such as he. I shall be glad to see him again, though.'

She bent to pat Bouncer, curled up at their feet. 'Jules brought Bouncer here while he is away; he's company for me and he does miss his master. Joop, too, comes here whenever I need him. Both my daughters live some distance away—Ineke in Goningen and Lisa in Limburg. They both have young children and homes to run, and it isn't easy for them to visit me very often. They telephone me several times a week, though.' She smiled. 'You see that I am very well cared for by my family.'

She put down her coffee cup. 'Would you like to see the rest of the house, Daisy? It will take some time, and then we can have a nice chat before tea.'

It certainly took time; Daisy could have spent hours lingering in the bedrooms. Especially the vast principal bedroom, with its four-poster and massive tallboy, and the dressing table under the bow windows, all of mahogany inlaid with tulip wood, and there was a silver ewer on a side-table which she would have liked to examine at her leisure. But politeness forced her to follow her hostess from room to room, some large, some small, all splendidly furnished.

'There are attics too,' explained Mevrouw der Huizma, 'crammed with more furniture, but that would take too long…'

She led the way downstairs, and as they reached the hall the doorbell clanged and Joop went to open the door.

'Who can that be?' She frowned. 'I was not expecting anyone to call.'

Certainly not Helene, who brushed past Joop and

crossed the hall, smiling, her hands held out as though she were about to embrace Mevrouw der Huizma.

'Mevrouw der Huizma. I come unannounced, but I thought we might have a talk together. You must be missing Jules and there is so much for us to discuss.'

Mevrouw der Huizma took one of the outstretched hands and shook it.

'Helene, this is a surprise. You have news of Jules?'

'Oh, just a note saying that he had arrived safely. I don't expect to hear from him, and really there's nothing of his work there which would interest me.'

'So I would imagine,' said Mevrouw der Huizma, and spoke in English. 'I believe that you have met Daisy at Jules's house?'

Helene gave Daisy a cursory glance. 'Have we? Oh, yes, you're the girl from the antique shop.' She added sharply, 'Are you looking over the furniture here?'

She was being deliberately rude, but Daisy ignored that. She didn't answer.

It was Mevrouw der Huizma who spoke. 'Daisy has spent the day with me.' She added deliberately, 'She has been here before, with Jules; he has shown her something of Holland while she is here.'

'Oh,' Helene's fine blue eyes were cold. While she

had been in California, of course. This nondescript girl had gone behind her back—though heaven knew what he saw in her. Something would have to be done about that, but not at the moment.

'You couldn't have a better person to show you the country,' she said, and smiled at Daisy. 'Are you going to be here long?'

'I'm not sure, but I expect I'll go home in another month or so. It depends on Heer Friske.'

They had walked as they talked, and now seated themselves in the drawing room. Helene curled up on one of the sofas, as if to demonstrate how at home she was. Bouncer went over to her, and she put out a beautifully shod foot and pushed him away. She laughed as she did it. 'Jules's awful dog—I'm always telling him that it should live in the kitchen. Has he given it to you?'

Mevrouw der Huizma said levelly, 'No, Bouncer stays with me while Jules is away. He is splendid company.'

'Well, I shall persuade Jules to give it to you when we marry. A dog is such a nuisance.'

Mevrouw der Huizma ignored that. 'Will you stay for tea? We are just about to have ours?'

'Just a cup of tea. I must lose a few pounds; I got positively fat while I was in California and I've brought some lovely clothes back with me so I don't dare to eat too much.' She gave a satisfied little laugh and looked down at the elegant outfit which emphasised the boniness of her person.

Flat as a board, reflected Daisy. That dress would look better on a coathanger. She felt better for the thought. She wasn't given to unkindness, but really Helene was a horrid woman, and how Jules could possibly want to marry her Daisy couldn't imagine. At the thought of him she smiled a little, and Helene, watching her, felt a little prickle of disquiet. What had the girl got to smile about? she asked herself with sudden suspicion. 'Has Jules written to you?'

'Me? No, why should he? I'm sure he's far too busy to write to anyone except his nearest and dearest.'

Helene pouted. 'Well, I think it is too bad of him to go off like this.'

Mevrouw der Huizma said quietly, 'But that is what you must expect if you are a medical man's wife, Helene.'

'Oh, I'm sure I shall be able to alter that once we are married. Jules has suggested that we marry soon, but there is no hurry. After all, I shall be spending the rest of my life as a housewife…'

Daisy wondered if she had any idea of how to be a housewife. True, she would know how to give orders to servants, but would she be a good wife and mother? It seemed unlikely. Daisy thought of the cold, unloving future lying in wait for Jules. Only perhaps he wouldn't notice that if he loved Helene.

She accepted a cup of tea from Mevrouw der Huizma and made polite conversation, reminding herself that loving Jules gave her no right to wish him to give up Helene. Thinking about it made her feel a little sick.

Helene showed no signs of leaving, and Daisy wondered if she should suggest that she herself should go back to Heer Friske's shop. But before she could think up a suitable excuse Mevrouw der Huizma observed, 'Daisy and I will be busy this evening. We are going to study the history of this house. There are any number of books, and diaries over a long period. Some of the invoices and bills are most interesting. They are housed in the attics and I dare say we shall get very dusty and chilly.' She smiled at Helene. 'Would you like to join us?'

'No—no, thank you. I'm going out to dinner and I must be leaving. If Daisy had been going back I could have offered her a lift…'

She made her farewells presently, and Mevrouw der Huizma said, 'Let me know if you have news of Jules…'

'Oh, I don't expect to. And I'm sure he won't have time to read letters from me.'

She glanced at Daisy, and Daisy held out a hand which was ignored.

When Helene was gone Mevrouw der Huizma said gently, 'I am sorry that Helene was rude, Daisy. Let us go upstairs to the attics and look around. I believe you may be interested.'

'I should go back…'

'Unless you wish to return to Heer Friske, I had hoped that you would have supper with me.'

'Oh. I'd like that very much. I thought that you said that about the attics…you know…' Daisy stopped and went red.

Mevrouw der Huizma laughed. 'In order that Helene might go away? Well, yes, but I had intended asking you to stay, my dear, so please do so. Joop shall drive you back after supper.'

They spent a delightful hour or so up under the gabled roof of the house, looking through the books and papers arranged on shelves in one of the larger attics.

'I seldom come up here now,' said Mevrouw der Huizma, 'but when my husband was alive we would spend hours up here.'

'It's fascinating,' said Daisy. 'Here's an invoice for a hundred-piece dinner service. There must have been a great deal of entertaining.'

'Undoubtedly. You must come again, Daisy, and look your fill. Now we will go downstairs for our supper.'

Mevrouw der Huizma dusted down her fine wool dress and led the way down.

Later that evening Joop drove Daisy back. It had been a lovely day; she had told her hostess so and had been warmly kissed.

'And we must repeat it,' Mevrouw der Huizma had said.

When Daisy had gone she sat down at her desk and wrote a letter to Jules, with Bouncer at her feet and the ginger cat sitting on her knee. As she wrote she wondered if Helene would write to him too; it seemed unlikely. Mevrouw der Huizma nibbled the end of her pen, frowning.

Helene had had no intention of writing to Jules; he had written briefly to her but she saw no point in answering his letter. She had no wish to know about his work, and the social life she so much enjoyed wouldn't interest him. He had tolerated her way of life, expecting her to change when they married—something which she'd had no intention of doing. But now, since her visit to his mother, she felt a faint doubt creeping into her complacency. Daisy, that dull girl, had wormed her way into Mevrouw der Huizma's graces, and was probably scheming to attract Jules. Of course, the idea was laughable, but one couldn't be too careful. Helene had no wish to marry him yet, life was pleasant as it was, but she must make sure that she held his interest…

So she wrote a long letter to Jules, with almost no mention of her own activities but containing an embellished version of her visit to his mother. Daisy, she wrote, had been there—such a sweet girl and so clever about antiques. She would be going back to England very shortly, and did Jules know that she was hoping to marry later in the year?

Helene was clever enough to write no more about Daisy; she had said just enough to make him forget the girl. She posted the letter and then made her plans. A little chat with Daisy would do no harm.

CHAPTER SEVEN

HALFWAY through the week Daisy was surprised to have a phone call from Helene, proposing that she should call for Daisy on Sunday and drive her to the sea. 'We can have lunch somewhere,' said Helene, 'and come back here for tea. Since you will be going back to England shortly, you must see as much as possible of Holland before then.'

Daisy was too taken aback to say anything for the moment. She didn't want to spend the day with Helene, but how could she refuse without seeming rude? Excuses flew through her head; none of them would hold water. She said finally, 'That would be delightful. Thank you, I'd like to come…'

'I'll call for you at eleven o'clock,' said Helene. 'Don't bother to dress up; we'll take pot luck.'

Since I've nothing to dress up in, thought Daisy, that need not worry me. I wonder why she is so friendly? Perhaps Jules had written to her and suggested it. But why would he do that? And surely Helene had a better way of spending her Sunday than driving her around, sightseeing? Especially as Daisy was only too well aware that Helene didn't like her.

Or perhaps I've misjudged her, thought Daisy, and felt guilty because of her dislike of the woman...

Helene arrived a little after eleven o'clock, driving a bright red sports car, wearing a white leather jacket over a red trouser suit. She looked lovely, and Daisy, getting into the car beside her, could quite see why Jules was in love with her. She hadn't got out of the car and had ignored Heer Friske and his wife waving from their living room window. Daisy looked up and waved as they sped away and hoped that they hadn't felt offended at Helene's indifference. But Helene was disposed to be friendly. 'Did Jules take you to Scheveningen? We'll go to Zandvoort first; we can have coffee there and then drive up the coast.'

Daisy, a little bewildered by this sudden show of friendliness, told herself that she had misjudged Helene, and readily answered her casually put questions.

'How fortunate that Jules was there to pull you out of the canal,' said Helene, 'and what a coincidence that you had already met. Did you see much of him in England?'

And Daisy, her doubts lulled by Helene's friendly manner, told her about their meeting, and the walk they had had along the shore. 'It was such a pleasant surprise to meet him again,' she said, and something in her voice made Helene look at her sharply. 'He has been very kind to me while I've been here.' She gave a little laugh. 'It's funny how we kept on meeting without meaning to.'

Helene, putting in a word here and there, encouraged her to talk. The girl was in love with Jules, that was obvious, and probably he had been flattered by that. Something which must be nipped in the bud before he got back to Amsterdam.

She had driven up the coast after they had had their coffee and presently stopped at Egmond-aan-Zee. She had deliberately chosen a rather splendid hotel, much frequented by the well-to-do and young, leisured men and women—something Daisy realised as they entered the restaurant. Her clothes were all wrong; she saw the faintly amused glances cast at her tweed jacket and skirt—adequate for Amsterdam, even if a bit wintry now, but here, amongst so many smartly dressed people, she stuck out like a sore thumb. She wished that Helene had chosen somewhere more modest as they were ushered to a table in the centre of the room, but Helene appeared not to see her unease.

'The menu is in French,' she said rather too loudly. 'Shall I translate for you?'

Daisy, whose French was more than adequate, felt a faint prickle of annoyance. Helene had seemed friendly, but now she was patronising her…

'I think I can manage,' Daisy said, and gave her order in nicely pronounced French, adding, 'We learn French in school, you know. I don't know why it should be French in preference to any other language.'

'I suppose it's considered necessary in a basic education.' A remark which Daisy told herself hadn't been intended unkindly.

She enjoyed her lunch. There was no point in allowing her surroundings to ruin her appetite.

They turned inland after leaving the hotel, to go through Alkmaar and cross to the other side of the country.

'You must see Vollendam,' said Helene. 'All the tourists go there; the villagers still wear the national costume. Of course it's a great attraction. Foreigners like to think of us wearing clogs.'

She stopped the car for a while so that Daisy could look around her and buy a postcard to send home.

'Of course, you're a tourist yourself,' remarked Helene, and laughed. 'You will have plenty to tell your family when you go back. Do you know when you are going?'

Helene had asked her that at Mevrouw der Huizma's house only a few days previously, and Daisy wondered why she was so eager to know.

'I haven't any idea. A few weeks, I dare say, perhaps longer.'

Helene didn't say any more, but then started talking about California and the fun she had had there.

A conversation which lasted until they were once more back in Amsterdam.

Once in the city, Helene drove away from its heart and Daisy said, 'I don't think I've been this way before. Is it a short-cut to Heer Friske's house?'

'No, no, we'll have tea at home and then I'll drive you back. It's still quite early and I'm sure you're longing for tea.'

'Well, that would be nice.' It would be interesting to see where Helene lived. In another lovely old house like Mr der Huizma's, perhaps.

Helene stopped outside a block of imposing flats in Churchillaan.

'Here we are.' She swept Daisy through the entrance guarded by a porter and got into the lift. 'We're on the second floor.'

The lift stopped and they walked along a wide carpeted corridor. Helene took out a key and opened a door at its end.

It was nothing like Mr der Huizma's house. There were vast rooms, heavily furnished, thickly carpeted, the windows swathed in vast curtains. Not an antique in sight. Helene led the way, opened double doors and urged her into the room beyond. There were two persons there, an elderly man and a woman somewhat younger. They both looked round as Helene and Daisy went in. Helene said something in Dutch and then added in English, 'This is Daisy, a girl Jules befriended on one or two occasions.'

She looked at Daisy. 'My parents, Daisy.'

Neither of them moved towards her. She took a step forward, a hand outstretched, and realised that neither of them intended to take it. She said, 'How do you do?' and waited to see who would speak first.

'Well, sit down,' said Mevrouw van Tromp. 'I expect you would like some tea. Ring the bell, Helene.' She stared at Daisy, her face devoid of expression.

'You are visiting here?'

'No. I work for Heer Friske, who has an antique shop.'

'Indeed, and why did you come to Amsterdam to work?'

'To gain experience…'

Helene had gone out of the room and came back without the leather jacket. 'Take your coat off, Daisy. It's getting rather warm for winter clothes. I don't suppose you have much, though. Do you go out at all?'

Daisy took off her jacket. She said quietly, 'No. I work all day, and in the evening I learn what I can about Dutch marquetry and china.'

Mevrouw van Tromp's voice was sharp. 'Do you work in a shop in England?'

Daisy said 'Yes, my father deals in antiques.'

'Indeed?' There was silence as tea was brought in.

Daisy was offered a cup of weak, milkless tea and a small biscuit, and while she nibbled at it she wondered if Mijhneer van Tromp was going to speak to her. Or was a shopgirl beneath his notice?

Mevrouw van Tromp sipped her tea. 'You have met Mr der Huizma?'

'Yes, several times, both here and in England.' Daisy nibbled again and wished she was anywhere other than where she was. Helene's parents were dreadful; how could Jules contemplate being their son-in-law? And this flat, almost vulgar in its ostentation. She supposed that if you loved someone well enough nothing else mattered…

She refused a second cup of tea and remarked, 'I've had a delightful day, Helene. Thank you for taking me for such a splendid trip. Would you mind taking me back to Heer Friske? We usually play bridge on Sunday evenings—a neighbour comes in and makes a fourth.'

Mevrouw van Tromp asked, 'You play bridge?' Her tone implied that shopgirls wouldn't know how.

Daisy had been holding her temper in check. Another remark like that and she might lose it. So she smiled and got up, and thanked her reluctant hostess for her tea and bade her goodbye. Mijhneer van Tromp still hadn't spoken, so she nodded to him and followed Helene back to her car.

Walking back to the flat's entrance, Helene said

over her shoulder, 'I expect it's all rather overwhelming…'

'Why should I be overwhelmed?'

'Such a difference in lifestyle. It must seem like another world to you.'

'No.' Daisy choked back the reply she would have liked to have made. 'I am aware of the difference, but it doesn't overwhelm me. Why should it?'

Helene said sweetly, 'Jules was afraid that you might feel awkward…' And, before Daisy could open her mouth to answer that one, 'We intend to marry within the next month or two. I did suggest that we might invite you to the wedding, but he is so thoughtful—it would mean a decent outfit—nothing off the peg—and there would be your fare here and a hotel—even the smaller hotels are expensive in Amsterdam.'

They had reached the door and got into the lift. 'You must think I'm horrid, saying things like this to you—' Helene sounded sincere '—but neither Jules nor I would want you to feel awkward.'

They were out in the street now. Daisy paused on the pavement. 'I'd like to walk back…'

'It's quite a long way…'

'But I like walking.' Daisy held out a hand. 'Such an interesting day,' she said, in a voice which revealed nothing of the surge of feelings threatening to burst from her person at any moment.

Helene hadn't expected that; she shook Daisy's hand and began, 'Oh, but…' But Daisy was already walking away. For the moment she was lost, but she looked as though she knew where she was going.

It took her some time to find her way back to Heer Friske's house. Mevrouw Friske was in the kitchen, arranging little biscuits on a dish. She looked up and smiled as Daisy went in, asked in her mixture of English and Dutch if Daisy had had a pleasant day, and added that there were five people coming presently to spend the evening. 'My sister and her husband and their three daughters. We shall enjoy a happy evening; there will be young people for you, Daisy.'

After Helene's barbed remarks, Mevrouw Friske's cosy voice was soothing. And the evening proved enjoyable too; the three girls, all about her own age, were friendly, their English a good deal better than Daisy's Dutch, and their skill at the card table was on a par with her own so that the bridge session was light-hearted.

As they wished her goodbye they voiced the hope that they would see more of her. It was Heer Friske who remarked that Daisy would be going back to England shortly. A remark which rather surprised her. She thought no more about it, though, but went to bed to go over and over in her mind Helene's remarks. Daisy knew that there had been no real friendliness on her part. Indeed, it was as if Helene had wanted to impress her with the difference in their lifestyles. She found it hard to believe that Jules had said the things Helene had told her, although she could see no reason for her to have lied about it. Possibly Jules had realised the difference in their way of life, but he would have meant it kindly, and he wouldn't have taken her to an ultra-smart restaurant if she had pointed out that her clothes were all wrong... Perhaps it was a good thing that he might not be back before she went home. Although to see him just once more was her dearest wish.

Where's your good sense? 'You're a silly girl,' Daisy told herself, 'to dream of Jules. Forget him and go to sleep.' Which eventually she did.

She went out in the morning to post her card home and poke around the row of small shops. She would buy presents to take home, but she wasn't sure what, and there was nothing there which she liked. She would beg a half-day from Heer Friske and go to the Kalverstraat. There was plenty of time to do that...

Only as it turned out there wasn't. Another week went by, and it was late the following Tuesday, when the last customer had finally gone after half an hour of browsing and buying nothing, that Heer Friske called her into his office.

He offered her a chair. 'We must have a talk,' he began. 'You have done well here, and I believe you have learned a lot. I had intended to ask you to stay until the end of the summer, but now a situation has arisen.'

He peered at her anxiously, but she returned his look placidly although she had a nasty suspicion of what was to come.

'Mevrouw Friske's niece—the eldest, Mel—you met her last week—she wishes very much to work for me, to be trained to a good knowledge of antiques. She has an aptitude already. And, as my wife says, it would be a good thing to have a member of the family working here in the shop, perhaps in time taking over when I retire. So, Daisy, she will replace you as soon as you wish to return to England. We have liked having you here with us, but you have a good home and a career before you. You must not think that we are turning you out; make your arrangements to suit yourself. We shall miss you; you have done well. I will write you an excellent recommendation. You do not mind that I say all this?'

He looked so upset that Daisy said at once, 'Of course not, Heer Friske. It's a splendid idea to have Mel work here with you. And I was going back home quite soon anyway, wasn't I? I've been very happy here and I've learnt a great deal. I'm grateful to you, and to Mevrouw Friske. When would Mel like to come? If I could have a day or two…'

He heaved a sigh of relief. 'If she should come on

Saturday, is that too soon for you? You may have as much free time as you need. You will want to get your ticket and perhaps say goodbye to friends.'

'That suits me very well. I haven't many friends, and I'll write to them or telephone. If I could have a few hours off to make arrangements?'

'Of course, and you will wish to telephone your parents. I also will speak to your father and explain. You do not find me unkind for doing this?'

He looked so woebegone that she leaned forward and kissed his cheek.

'You're one of the kindest men I've ever met,' she told him.

She would fly back, she decided, and her father would meet her at Heathrow. She had very little luggage, and getting to Schipol would be quick and easy.

She booked on the Friday morning flight, spent a morning shopping—cigars for her father, a silk scarf for her mother—and she wrote a letter to Mevrouw der Huizma. It was brief and stilted, for it was difficult not to mention Jules. She thanked her again for the pleasant visits she had paid, sent her love to Bouncer, expressed her pleasure at returning home and sent good wishes.

She would have liked to have said goodbye personally, but it was better this way; to go away quietly and be the more easily forgotten.

Saying goodbye to the Friskes wasn't easy. She had grown to like Heer Friske and his wife, but, as she told herself over and over again, it was a good thing that she was leaving Amsterdam. She was leaving Jules and all her dreams too, but that was another matter. Out of sight, out of mind, Daisy told herself stoutly, and, clutching the carefully wrapped china figurine Heer Friske had pressed into her hands at the last minute, she got into the taxi.

A bus took her to Schipol, and as she got out of it she was momentarily taken aback by the size of the place. She went through the entrance and found its vast reception area teeming with people. Unlike her, they all appeared to know where they were going. She had plenty of time, she told herself, and stood for a moment reading the signs and directions, rotating slowly, anxious not to miss something vital. She must go to the left; she checked that she had her ticket ready and picked up her case, and then put it down again as she saw Mr der Huizma coming towards her.

She should have pretended not to see him, picked up her case and lost herself in the crowds… She stood waiting for him to reach her, schooling her face to polite surprise.

'What are you doing here? And why have you a case with you?'

He hadn't said hullo, or bothered with some conventional remark about meeting her again.

'I'm catching a plane home,' said Daisy, quite giddy with delight at seeing him just once more. He seemed larger than ever, and although he was as immaculately dressed as always he looked tired and somehow older.

'Was it awful?' asked Daisy. 'And were you able to help?'

'Yes and yes.' He smiled at her then. 'Why are you leaving, Daisy?'

'I'm going home,' she told him again. 'I must go and get my boarding pass or I shall miss the plane.'

'But you had a reason to leave?' he persisted.

She blushed, but didn't avoid his eye. 'I've learnt a lot and I've enjoyed living here. Heer Friske has a niece who is going to take my place in the shop…'

'That is the only reason? Did you visit my mother?'

'Yes, I had a lovely day with her. And Helene took me out for a Sunday—it was kind of you to ask her to do that. We had a most interesting day.'

His face hadn't altered, but she thought that he was angry. 'I really must go. Father will be waiting for me at Heathrow.'

She offered a hand and he ignored it, but gathered her in his arms and kissed her. As far as Daisy was concerned, Schipol had become paradise, planes and an anxious parent and boarding cards meant nothing.

He let her go slowly and gently, picked up her case and took her arm.

'You'll need to go along here.' He sounded as calm as usual—perhaps she had dreamt that kiss…

She joined the queue and got her pass and he handed her case over.

'Over there. I can't come any further.'

'No, no, of course not. Thank you. Goodbye!'

He put out a hand and touched her cheek. 'Have a safe journey,' was all he said.

She joined another queue and didn't look round, and presently she was on the plane and Holland was far below, giving way to the North Sea and presently to the English coast.

Heathrow was as busy as Schipol, but had the advantage of English signs and directions. She found her way without difficulty to the entrance and found her father waiting.

He wasn't a demonstrative man, but he was delighted to see her again and she was glad to see him, for she loved him very dearly. She would never be able to tell him or her mother about Mr der Huizma, but they both loved her and with them she would go back to her quiet life and in time Holland would be a distant dream. She gave her father a tremendous hug. 'It's so nice to be home again,' she told him.

There was much to tell them when she got home, and there was no need to mention Jules's name—although she did tell them about her visits to Mevrouw der Huizma's house.

'And did you see much of the doctor?' asked her mother.

Daisy said steadily, 'Very occasionally. He was kind enough to drive me around on one or two Sundays, so that I could see a little of Holland. Oh, and we met by accident…' She recounted the incident of the old lady and her cat and they all laughed about it, but something in her face made her mother give her a sharp glance. There were shadows under Daisy's eyes, and from time to time she looked sad…

Once she had settled in again, there was plenty to keep Daisy busy. Her father had bought a quantity of early Victorian furniture, in perfect condition but woefully uncared for. It fell to Daisy's lot to clean the heavy chairs and cabinets and what-nots, then polish them to perfection. She was glad to have something to do, and spent long, patient hours in the small room at the back of the shop with soft brushes and cloths and the special polish her father made for himself. At the end of two weeks or so she had finished, and some of the furniture was put on display. Her father, arranging a balloon-back chair in the window, paused to look at Daisy, giving a final polish to a walnut Davenport, and thought uneasily that he had been working her too hard; she was pale and rather quiet.

Later, as they were having their lunch, he said, 'You've been working too hard for the last week or two, Daisy. I've been so anxious to have that furniture ready to sell that I haven't given you a moment to yourself. You're quite pale, my dear. You must have more free time. How about starting those walks of yours again? Morning or afternoon—whichever you'd rather have.'

'But there are quite a few customers…'

'Mostly in the afternoon. The browsers and tourists come in the mornings, but they never stay long and buy only the small stuff.'

'Then I'll go in the morning, Father. I'd like that. If I go after breakfast I'll be back well before lunchtime.' She added, 'And if we get really busy I won't go.'

'It seems as though you've never been away,' said her mother, 'and you've been home almost three weeks.'

Three weeks since I saw Jules, thought Daisy, and she seemed quite unable to forget him, even banish him to the back of her mind. If he hadn't kissed her it might have been easier…

Mr der Huizma had watched Daisy's small person until she was out of sight and then gone out into the street where Joop had been waiting with the car. He'd greeted him pleasantly, enquired after his health and the well-being of his household, not forgetting Bouncer, and taken the wheel.

'Bad, was it?' asked Joop, with the respectful familiarity of an old and devoted servant. 'You'll need a bit of a holiday, *mijnheer*.'

'Yes, it was bad, but not quite as bad now as when I arrived there. As for a holiday, that must wait until I've got my work organised here.'

Joop glanced at his master's profile. It looked grim and there were tired lines. He decided not to mention that Juffrouw van Tromp had phoned to ask when the doctor was returning. She wanted to know, she'd explained to Joop, so that she could arrange a party for him. 'So let me know immediately,' she had ordered sharply. Joop had done nothing of the sort; he had had a message from his master that very day, and if he hadn't chosen to let his fiancée know that wasn't Joop's business.

Joop frowned as they crawled through the city's traffic. Juffrouw van Tromp wasn't at all to his liking, nor to anyone else in Mr der Huizma's house.

Once more in his home, Mr der Huizma greeted Jette and Bouncer, and then went to his study to go through his pile of post and make several telephone calls. That done, he went to his room, showered and changed and came downstairs to find coffee waiting for him.

He sat drinking it, thinking of Daisy. He wasn't sure if she'd been pleased to see him; she had been surprised, of course, just as he had been, but she had been on edge to go. He had tried to detect any sign of pleasure at seeing him but her face had shown nothing but polite surprise. He told himself that he should be glad of that; in the face of her indifference to him he could put her out of his mind.

He went back to his study and settled down to work his way through the papers on his desk. And after lunch he returned to his study once more, to phone his mother before resuming work.

He had told Joop to let his mother know that he was coming home, and there had been a message from her saying that she would be back from visiting one of his sisters shortly after lunch. When he dialled the number she answered at once.

'Jules, you're back. I'm so thankful. You're busy, of course, but when you can spare an hour come and see me. Was it bad?'

He told her a little of his work, and added, 'I'm going to be busy for several days, Mother, but I'll come and see you just as soon as I can.' And, unable to help himself, he added, 'I saw Daisy at Schipol, going home.'

'Yes, dear. I had a letter saying she was leaving

Holland. Her reasons seemed vague. Did you have time for a talk?'

'No. A couple of minutes only. Are you well?'

So Daisy wasn't to be talked about. 'Very well, dear. Don't let me keep you gossiping; I'm sure you're busy enough.'

He ate a solitary dinner presently, took Bouncer for a walk and went back to his study. Not to work, but to contemplate a future which for him held no happiness. He had every intention of going over to England and seeing Daisy. There was no question of forgetting her. He had fallen in love with her, and he loved her, and he wanted her for his wife. If she could love him a little he would ask Helene to release him...

He had forgotten Helene; it was too late to go and see her, or even phone her. He would have to go to the hospital in the morning but the afternoon should be free. They could talk; they hadn't talked for a long time. Dining, meeting at friends' houses, going to a play had never offered the opportunity to talk.

He forgot his own problems once he entered the hospital the next morning. He became immersed in his little patients' problems, and the afternoon was well advanced by the time he got home to eat a late lunch and then get into his car and drive to Churchillaan.

Juffrouw van Tromp was home, the correct maid

told him, and led the way to the drawing room. At the door he said, 'No, don't announce me,' and went quietly in.

Helene was there, sitting on one of the overstuffed sofas, talking to a man he didn't know. She saw him first and jumped to her feet, flustered, but covering it with cries of delighted surprise.

'Jules—you're back. What an unexpected—'

He cut her short. 'Yesterday. How are you, Helene?' He glanced at the man who had got to his feet.

'This is Hank Cutler—we met when I was in California. He's over here on business and came to see me. Hank, this is Jules der Huizma, my fiancé.'

She had recovered her usual air of casual sophistication and added, 'Come and sit down, Jules. I'm so glad you have come; we were discussing the party I was planning to welcome you back.'

Mr der Huizma stood quietly, not speaking, and Hank got to his feet again. 'I have to be going; you must have a lot to say to each other. Been in Africa, haven't you? Must have been interesting…'

'Interesting if one likes to watch small children and babies die,' said Mr der Huizma. A remark which sped Hank on his way.

When he had gone Helene said angrily, 'Really, Jules, did you have to be so pompous?'

She was looking very beautiful, exquisitely turned

out, her make-up faultless, and anger had heightened her beauty.

'My apologies.' He sat down. 'I must learn to keep my opinions to myself.'

'Yes, you must,' she said sharply, 'if they are miserable ones—upsetting my friends.' She grumbled, 'I dare say he won't come to my party now.'

'I dare say I won't either!' said Jules smoothly. 'What have you been doing with yourself while I've been away?'

'I had a week at that hydro—really, I was exhausted. And there was that exhibition I told you about—everyone was there—and of course shopping is so tiring... Oh, and I had tea with your mother. That girl Daisy was there, looking at your furniture, or so she said. I don't trust these quiet girls—worming her way into your mother's good books...'

He said quietly, 'Why should she do that?'

'Ambitious, I dare say, hoping to get something, or get someone like your mother interested in her. I took her out for the day—thought I would let her see how different her world was from ours.' Helene gave him a defiant look. 'I told her that we were going to get married within the next month or so.'

And when he didn't answer, she added, 'Well, before you went away you seemed anxious to get married...'

'And are you? Anxious?' He sounded casual, and he looked positively placid.

Helene said slowly, 'Since you ask, no, I can't see that there is any hurry. You have your work and I have my friends. In the autumn, if you like.'

He asked idly, 'Why did you take Daisy out for the day?'

She laughed. 'I told her that you had asked me to do so. I said that you wanted her to have a treat before she went home.'

'Why did you say that?' His voice was quiet but she frowned a little at the look on his face. 'Oh, I suppose I wanted her to realise that she wasn't one of us. I think she enjoyed herself; she told me all about this faithful boyfriend waiting for her to say yes.'

She gave him a quick look. He had minded that. She felt sudden fury that he should have been interested in such a dull girl when she herself was a woman everyone admired, who was lovely to look at, exquisitely dressed, fun to be with, a splendid hostess… She said, with a flash of anger, 'Oh, forget about her, Jules. She was one of those girls clever enough to know how to better themselves.'

He got to his feet. 'You're wrong, Helene. Daisy, was—is—someone you don't often come across. She was kind and honest and warm-hearted. Beauty is only skin-deep, you know.'

That frightened Helene. She crossed the room to him and put her arms round his neck. 'Oh, Jules, I don't mean half I say—you know that. I hope she will be very happy now that she is back with her young man. We'll send her a wedding present.' She smiled charmingly at him. 'Take time off, darling, let's go somewhere and celebrate. I'm really sorry; don't hate me for it. We'll marry at once if you want.' She looked into his face. 'You do want that, don't you, Jules?'

He looked at her lovely face. 'I've a backlog of work. I'd rather not make plans for a time.'

She had to be content with that, and after he had gone she wondered if her future was as secure as she had supposed it to be. She would take care not to mention Daisy again. Out of sight, out of mind, Helene decided, and, going to take a look at her reflection in the wall mirror, felt confident that she could arrange her life as she wanted it.

As for Mr der Huizma, he went back home to sit at his desk and study the days ahead; it would be a while before he could be free for two or three days. Time enough to go over to England and see Daisy.

CHAPTER EIGHT

ON THE Sunday evening Mr der Huizma went to see his mother. He had dealt with the most urgent aspects of his work at the hospital and now got into his car once more and drove to his family home. He was still tired, and although he greeted her with his usual warmth he looked stern. Something was worrying him, and she thought that it was something other than his experiences in Africa. But she said nothing, and told him to pour himself a drink and sit down and tell her of his mission. It took some time, for she was interested and interrupted frequently. He fell silent at last. 'It was good to be able to talk about it,' he told her.

At supper they talked about the family, and finally his work. 'I suppose you will be busy now for the next few weeks,' said his mother.

'Yes, but I intend to take a couple of days off as soon as I can manage it. I'm going to England.' He glanced at his mother. 'To see Daisy.'

So that was the reason for his stern face. 'Yes, dear. She came here and spent the day. We had a delightful time up in the attics. It was a pity that Helene called—we had to leave some most interesting old books about this house. I had hoped to invite her again, but of course she returned rather suddenly to England.'

'Did she say why?'

'Heer Friske had a niece who wanted to join his business. It was a short note; I had the impression that it wasn't the usual kind of letter she would have written. I telephoned Heer Friske. He sounded really sorry that she had gone home, and observed that she had at least seen something of Holland before she went. Helene took her out for the day—perhaps you knew that?'

'Helene told me. She also told me that she had told Daisy that we were to marry very shortly.'

Mevrouw der Huizma said slowly, 'And are you, Jules? Going to marry soon?'

'No. It seems that Helene told Daisy that for reasons of her own. She has no wish to marry in the foreseeable future.'

His mother breathed a hidden sigh of relief. 'Well, dear, since you are so busy for weeks ahead that might be a good idea.'

He said harshly, 'Was Daisy happy? Here in this house with you?'

'Yes, Jules. And a delightful companion. A clever girl, I fancy, able to hold her own in any situation and, to use an old-fashioned word, modest about her knowledge.'

They began to talk of other things, and Daisy wasn't mentioned again.

Jules went back to Amsterdam. He would phone his mother before he went to England, he told her.

She sat, long after he had gone, thinking about him. He was a grown man, capable of running his own life, and had indeed made a success of it. She dared not meddle. He would do what was right, she was sure of that, but at what cost to his happiness? There was always the chance that Helene would release him from his promise, but she had to admit that it was a slim one.

And she was right; Helene, anxious now that she had lost whatever love Jules had had for her, did everything she could to recapture it. She did it in the only way she knew how; phoning him in the evenings, asking him to join her at some friend's house for dinner, suggesting that they should drive out into the country and dine at some popular restaurant, go to a play, spend a Sunday at Keukenhof, laughing off his protests that he had no time to spare. So from time to time he spent an evening with her, a pleasant companion listening to her chatter, admiring her dresses. That there was no warmth in his manner didn't worry her. She was an undemonstrative woman, not capable of loving deeply. She was confident that in time she would be able to arrange their future exactly as she wanted it.

It was a shock when he told her one evening that he would be going to England in a few days' time.

'To one of the hospitals?'

'I have two hospitals to visit, yes. I am going to see Daisy.'

She managed to keep her face composed. 'Give her my love. I dare say she is getting ready for her wedding. Perhaps you could find time to get her a present from us?'

'I doubt that.' He began to talk of something else then.

Daisy, now that summer was here, made the most of her daily walks. In another few weeks her father would need her more often in the shop, and her outings would have to be curtailed, even stopped for the height of the tourist season. She had a little colour in her cheeks now, but she had grown thinner and there were violet shadows under her eyes. But although she was quiet she was unendingly cheerful. That she longed to see Jules was something she kept to herself. She talked readily enough about her stay in Holland but Jules she never mentioned, something her mother had noticed with a troubled heart.

It was a bright, blustery day when she set out for her usual walk, but the sky was blue, even if overshadowed from time to time by great billowing clouds. She put on a cardigan over the sober dress she wore in the shop, tied a scarf over her neat head, and set out. She was a little later than usual, for her father had asked her to clean and polish a small silver-framed hand mirror; a delicate trifle which, arranged in the window, would draw the attention of passers-by. She would take her usual walk, she decided, go as far as the tumble of rocks at the far end of the beach and then climb the short distance to the coast path and go home along the low cliffs.

She was halfway to the rocks when she saw someone coming towards her. He had a dog with him, Trigger, who lumbered up to meet her with delighted barks. Daisy stood still. If she could have run away she would have done so, despite the happy beating of her heart at the sight of the vast figure coming so rapidly towards her. But there was nowhere to run…

He had reached her before she had her breathing under control. She said, inanely, 'It's a lovely day.'

He smiled slowly. 'The loveliest day of my life.'

'How funny that we've met again here on the beach.' She bent to pat Trigger, trying to get her self-possession back, wishing she could think of a few sensible remarks to make, casual and rather cool…

She need not have bothered; he said briskly, 'It's such a splendid day for a walk, isn't it? Are you going as far as the rocks?'

And when she nodded he said, 'Then may I join you? I'm over here for a few days and am giving myself a short break between hospitals. How are you liking being back home?'

He was friendly, with the casual friendliness of an old acquaintance, and Daisy fell into step beside him, torn between delight at seeing him once again and regret that he had shown no great pleasure at meeting her once more. Well, why should he? she asked herself silently, skipping to keep up. He had Helene... To maintain a conversation was essential, so she asked about his work in Africa.

He told her at some length, knowing that she was interested and listening to what he was saying, now and then making intelligent observations. But presently he said, 'Now it's your turn, Daisy. What are your plans for the future?'

She answered him seriously. 'Well, it's funny you should ask—we were talking about it this morning. In fact we've talked about it quite a lot lately, but nothing is decided.'

She didn't say more than that. Why should he be interested in her plan to get taken on by one of the big firms dealing in antiques so that she might learn even more? She thought that perhaps she had been rather abrupt and added, 'Of course it would mean father would have to get an assistant.'

A fragmented and misleading remark which left Mr der Huizma no better informed than he had been. But he was a man of infinite patience and he was here for another two days. He began to talk about nothing in particular in his friendly way, and Daisy, blissfully happy for the moment, threw sticks for Trigger, her face rosy from the wind, uncaring of the tendrils of hair escaping from her scarf. Somehow it didn't matter how she looked when she was with Jules. And anyway, he wasn't really looking at her—a quick glance from time to time, that was all.

They had reached the rocks, and she would have liked nothing better than to climb round them and go on walking, but it would soon be midday and she was to take over the shop that afternoon. She said urgently, 'I must go back…'

'The morning is quickly over,' he said easily. They didn't say much on their way back, and at the corner of the lane he bade her goodbye. She longed to know if he would meet her again, but, Daisy being Daisy, she didn't say anything, just bade him goodbye in her turn and ran to the shop and went inside without looking back.

Helping her mother lay the table for their lunch, she reflected that it was a good thing they wouldn't meet again. Perhaps it would have been better if they hadn't met this morning, upsetting all her efforts to put him out of her mind…

'Did Mr der Huizma find you?' asked her father as they sat at table. Daisy, caught unawares, went a bright pink although she sounded composed.

'Yes, Father, it was pleasant seeing him again. He's here for a day or two...'

And her mother said, 'He was so kind to you while you were in Holland...'

Daisy didn't want him to be kind; she wanted him to love her...

She thought about him during the afternoon, waiting patiently while a customer dithered between a Sèvres plate and a Rockingham milk jug. Would he be on the beach tomorrow? she wondered. He had said goodbye without saying that they might meet again. She would take her usual walk, she decided as she wrapped up the milk jug. Their meeting had been by chance, and if he had wanted to see her again he would have said so.

He was there, waiting at the bottom of the steps on the sea front, Trigger weaving happily to and fro. His good morning was cheerfully friendly as they started off towards the rocks. 'But I believe we're in for some bad weather,' he added.

She glanced uneasily at the sky. It was clear overhead, but out to sea the clouds were grey and threatening.

'Do you suppose these clouds are coming this way?'

'Yes, I'm afraid so. Perhaps you would rather go home?'

'No. No. I like the rain, only sometimes we get really bad weather here.'

They were walking side by side, content in each other's company, and Mr der Huizma looked at her small face, rosy from the wind, and thought how beautiful she was. 'Well,' he said, 'if you don't mind the rain…'

The clouds didn't appear to be moving and the wind had died down; they walked briskly, not saying much. There was still a day left, he reflected, and until then he was determined to remain nothing but a casual friend. But tomorrow he must ask her about the future—this man she was to marry. She wasn't wearing a ring…

They were almost at the rocks when he glanced out to sea. The sky had darkened but they hadn't noticed; now the clouds which had been hovering on the horizon were creeping towards them. His eyes narrowed.

'I'm not sure, but I think there's bad weather coming fast. We can sit it out among the rocks.' He whistled to Trigger and took her hand.

He had explored the rocks several times and knew where to go, between two great outcrops facing inland. Almost there, Daisy stopped to look out to sea. 'Oh, look,' she cried. 'Isn't that extraordinary…?'

'A whirlwind,' said Mr der Huizma calmly. 'Most

interesting. But come along now.' He had Trigger on his lead and a vast arm round Daisy.

They settled with their backs to the rock which encircled them and Daisy asked, 'Will it last long, the whirlwind?'

'No. A bit noisy and rough, but we're secure here. I'm sorry; I should have seen it earlier.'

Daisy, feeling his arm around her, was glad that he hadn't.

It grew darker and noisier, and all at once the whirlwind was upon them—and gone again before Daisy had the time to feel frightened. But it was followed by great peals of thunder and flashes of lightning. She had always been frightened of storms; now she buried her face in his shoulder and kept her eyes tight shut.

She muttered into his Burberry, 'I'm terrified of storms. So sorry.'

She was surprised to hear his rumble of laughter, but all he said was, 'It will soon pass. We're quite safe here.'

Positively cosy, reflected Daisy, her head on his shoulder, Trigger's doggy warmth pressed up against her legs… She swallowed down her fright and thought how happy she was, sitting here hidden from the storm and Jules's arm holding her close. There was a great deal of him, and he was very solid. This, she thought, was a moment to remember for the rest of her life.

The whirlwind had passed, the storm was blowing itself out, and the thunder was a rumble in the distance. Jules took his arm away and stood up. It was raining, but there was a clear sky out to sea where the last of the clouds were hurtling away.

He hauled her to her feet, took her arm and walked her briskly back along the beach, Trigger walking soberly beside them. It was raining still, and the sea was boisterous, but Daisy, happy in her own particular heaven, didn't notice. Mr der Huizma, looking down at her blissful face, sighed and wished for a miracle. To break his promise to marry Helene wasn't a thing he would contemplate, but surely there was some way in which she might decide that to marry him was a mistake?

'I'm going back to Holland tomorrow evening,' he told her as they climbed the steps to the promenade. 'Could you get a few hours off? We might drive into the country and have lunch?'

She stood beside him amidst the litter the whirlwind had caused. 'Well, I usually walk for a bit each morning, but I go to the shop after lunch…'

'Then if I call for you around ten o'clock we could lunch early and have you back in good time.'

'I'd like that—if I could be back here before two o'clock…'

'That's a promise.'

He walked with her up the main street and waited at the corner of the lane until she had gone into the shop. She hadn't looked back.

For Daisy the rest of the day was endless; she washed her hair, did her nails, pleased in a modest way that she had pretty hands, inspected her face for spots, and went to bed early—but not to sleep immediately. The morning's events had to be gone over; every word, every smile!

She saw with pleasure in the morning that the weather was on her side; hardly a cloud, and warm enough for her to wear the jersey dress. She was ready long before ten o'clock, but all the same when she heard the car stop outside she stayed in her room until her mother called her. Mr der Huizma was in the living room, looking very much at home, discussing the weather. His, 'Good morning, Daisy,' was pleasant, but if her mother was looking for any warmer feeling she was to be disappointed. He was a man who had complete control over his features—an asset in his profession.

'Where are we going?' asked Daisy as he got into the car beside her.

'Dartmoor. I've booked a table at Gidleigh Park, just outside Chagford. They will give us lunch at half past twelve, which gives us plenty of time to get back by two o'clock.'

He took the road to Two Bridges, and then on to Postbridge, stopping for coffee at a small café there and driving unhurriedly along the narrow roads, pausing to watch the ponies and sheep with their lambs.

'Oh, this is lovely,' said Daisy as they sat in the car, patiently waiting for a ewe and her lambs to cross the road.

'Would you like to walk for a while?'

'Oh, yes, but is there time?'

'We can spare twenty minutes or so. We can go as far as that tor…'

The sun was warm and the air fresh; they walked briskly, and after a minute, since the rough grass was awkward to walk on, he took her hand. To Daisy, her fingers curled into his large palm, it seemed the most natural thing in the world to do.

Gidleigh Park was a hotel close to Chagford, in its own splendid grounds with the North Teign river running through them. It was an elegant place, offering unostentatious luxury and delicious meals. They had a table by one of the windows in the half-filled restaurant; the tables close to them were, as yet, empty. Daisy studied the menu and gulped back shock at the prices. Mr der Huizma, watching her face, said matter-of-factly, 'Shall I choose for you, or is there something you would particularly like?'

'Oh, yes, please, you choose…' She added with the unselfconsciousness of a child, 'I'm hungry.'

'Good, so am I. How about spinach tarts, lamb cutlets, and choose our pudding from the trolley?'

The tarts were delicious, and the cutlets came with new potatoes, baby carrots, petit pois and broccoli.

'Heavenly,' said Daisy, daintily polishing off the last of the carrots.

The pudding trolley was something to drool over. She chose chocolate mousse laced with brandy and topped with cream, accompanied by small paper-thin biscuits, while Mr der Huizma ate cheese.

Pouring coffee for them both, she beamed across the table at him.

'I'm having such a glorious day…'

He took his cup from her. 'Daisy, I am in love with you, do you know that?'

She put her coffee cup very carefully back into the saucer. She felt the colour creep into her face but she gave him a direct look.

'I didn't know, but I had begun to wonder if you were. I've tried not to think about it. You're going to marry Helene—quite soon, she told me.' She steadied her voice. 'It's because we keep meeting unexpectedly, don't you see? I mean, falling in the canal and being mugged and helping me with the wine cooler and…' She stared at his quiet face. 'If you saw me every day you wouldn't even notice me.'

When he still didn't speak she went on desperately, 'You're going back to Holland tonight; we shan't see each other again and you'll forget me.'

He said then, 'And that is what you would like? That I should forget you?'

When she nodded, he added, 'Well, it is a most sensible suggestion and, given the circumstances, the right one. We are both of us tied by circumstances, are we not?'

He smiled at her, looking quite unworried, so that she asked, 'But we're still friends?'

'Of course. I can't imagine that Helene or your future husband could object to that. Especially as our friendship will be of necessity a long distance one.'

'My future husband? I haven't got one. I mean no one has ever asked me to marry them.' She stared at him.

A slow smile spread over Mr der Huizma's handsome features. 'I was told that you were to marry shortly—some young man here.'

'I don't know any young men,' said Daisy. 'Desmond was the only one, and I can't even remember what he looked like…'

She looked at Mr der Huizma and thought that he looked ten years younger all at once.

'There is a great deal that I should like to say,' he

told her. 'But it must wait for the moment. This has been a most illuminating conversation, Daisy.'

'Well, yes, but you do understand about you and me? I'm sure that once you get back to Amsterdam you'll have so many other things to think about—getting married…'

'Ah, yes. Now that is something about which I must think very seriously.'

He looked so cheerful, almost smug. Perhaps he was already falling out of love with her—and indeed there was nothing lover-like in his manner. She reflected sadly that his falling in love with her had been a moment's fantasy. A pity that she couldn't dismiss her own love for him with the same ease.

They went back to the car presently, and drove back along the main roads. Mr der Huizma chatted about this and that, for all the world as though he had never said that he was in love with her…

At the shop he got out with her, stayed to chat for a while with her mother and father, and then bade them goodbye. Good manners took her to the door with him.

'I hope you have a good journey home,' she said quietly. 'Please remember me to your mother and Helene. And thank you for a lovely morning and my lunch.' And then, 'Oh, Jules…'

This was what he had wanted to hear—the sudden longing in her voice. Her stoic front of friendliness was just that—a front. But he didn't say anything, only took her in his arms and kissed her. A long, slow kiss full of tenderness and love. Neither did he say goodbye, but got into his car and drove away without a backward glance.

And Daisy, regardless of the fact that she should be in the shop, went to her room and cried her eyes out. When she had no more tears left she washed her face, tidied her hair and went down to the shop, red-eyed, but perfectly composed, and sold a Victorian chamber pot, a walnut what-not and a warming pan to successive customers.

Her enthusiasm for work astonished her father, who put it down to her pleasure at being back in England but her mother wasn't deceived.

'Do you suppose that you will hear from Mr der Huizma again, dear?' she asked casually several days later. 'I dare say he will send you a wedding card or something similar. After all you did know his fiancée, didn't you?'

'Not very well, Mother. I don't expect to hear from either of them. They have so many friends of their own.' Daisy took an apple from the dish on the table and bit into it—it was something to do, and would perhaps divert her mother from questioning her. But Mrs Gillard didn't ask any more questions; she was sure that Daisy was unhappy, and that Mr der Huizma was the cause of it. A pity she had ever gone to Amsterdam… Mrs Gillard loved her daughter dearly, and longed to see her happy again.

Daisy, aware of this, did her best. But sometimes when she looked in a mirror she wondered how it was possible to look exactly the same as usual when one's heart was broken.

Mr der Huizma had gone back to Amsterdam, phoned his mother to tell her that he was back, but had made no effort or plans to phone or meet Helene. He was extremely busy, and he needed time to find ways and means whereby he could sort out his future. At the moment he could think of nothing, but that didn't deter him from his determination. Daisy loved him, he was sure of that now, and she held his heart in her hands. That was enough for him for the moment. He put her out of his mind and concentrated on his small patients.

His ward was full, it always was, and his clinics were larger than ever. He kept his mind on his work until some ten days after his return, when he had the time to go and see Helene. He had seen none of his friends, not even his mother, and had immersed himself so deeply in his work that Joop took it upon himself to remonstrate with him. 'Work yourself into an early grave,' he predicted. 'Not an hour's leisure have you had, excepting for taking Bouncer for his walk. It's not natural.'

'Don't worry, Joop, I intend to visit Juffrouw van Tromp this evening,' he had replied. Which satisfied his old servant but not entirely. Ten days his master had been home and not so much as a phone call from the lady. Joop shook his head and went along to the kitchen to discuss his doubts with Jette.

As it happened there was a phone call from Helene waiting for Jules on his answering machine when he got home. She had just heard that he had been back home for ten days, so why hadn't he been to see her or at least telephoned? But, since he was home again, perhaps he could spare the time to see her that evening. He listened to the cross voice and admitted that she had reason to be annoyed. He picked up the phone and dialled her number.

He wasn't free early enough in the evening to take her out to dinner. 'I shall be having drinks with friends and dining with them. You'd better come about nine o'clock. There are several parties during the next week or so and I've accepted for both of us; I'll let you know the dates. And don't be late. I have to be up early—I'm going to Amersfoort for the weekend with the de Groots.'

She rang off and he went to the dinner table and ate the excellent meal set before him. He took Bouncer for a walk, and then got into his car and drove to Churchillaan. Helene was waiting for him in the ornate drawing room.

'So here you are at last. Why wasn't I told that you were back?' She offered a cheek and he kissed it briefly.

'If you had phoned the hospital or my house, you would have been told,' he said mildly.

'My dear Jules, I can't spend my time on the phone; you know how full my days are.'

'My days are full too.' He sat down opposite her. She had thrown herself down on a sofa and she looked very beautiful.

'Well, don't be so gloomy. Wait while I tell you about these parties...'

'While I was in England I went to see Daisy. Helene, why did you tell me that she was to be married? A joke? A mistake?'

'A joke, of course. A girl like Daisy hasn't a chance of marrying—no looks, no decent clothes, her nose buried in old furniture.' Helene looked at him sharply. 'Anyway, she's back where she belongs; you can forget her.'

She realised that she hadn't got his full attention and had a moment of panic. Had someone told him that she'd been seeing rather a lot of Hank Cutler? She said sweetly, 'She is such a nice girl. Really I'm sure she'll find a husband. Now tell me, Jules, have you been busy at the hospital? Have you had any news of that new clinic you started in Africa?'

She could be charming when she wished, and she

exerted every scrap of that now. 'Shall we have coffee and I'll tell you about the parties I've promised we'll go to.' She saw his frown. 'At any rate I've promised for myself, but I said that you would come with me if you were free...'

He saw that the African clinic and his work there were already forgotten. He said quietly, 'I think it is unlikely that I shall be free for much social life for some time to come.'

'You're not going back to that clinic, Jules? I won't allow it. You've only been back a few weeks; you should be here, free to escort me, take me out to dinner, meet my friends...'

His eyes were cold. 'Did you not realise when we became engaged that I am not always free to do as I choose? Children are taken ill at the most inconvenient times; they don't wait until I am at the hospital to break arms and legs, scald themselves or fall ill for no reason at all.'

He had spoken in his usual calm way but she saw that he was angry. It wouldn't do at all; she would lose her hold over him.

'Jules, dear, I don't mean to be so thoughtless. Of course your work must come first. I promise you that I'll be a model wife. I'll entertain for you, so that you meet all the most influential people. I'm so proud of you, and I want you to be famous world-wide, not just here and in Europe. I shall be such a help to you.'

She talked on, but Mr der Huizma wasn't listening, nor did he see Helene lying so beguilingly on the sofa opposite him. All he saw in his mind's eye was a quiet girl with beautiful eyes and a quantity of brown hair…

It would have been useless to talk to Helene about their future at that moment. He would have to wait until she was in a more serious mood, get her to listen to him. She was still talking about parties and the wonderful weekend she hoped to have, and when he got up to go she stayed on the sofa, knowing what a delightful picture she made, and held out a hand.

'I'm far too tired to get up, Jules!' She smiled up at him. 'Phone me when you have a free evening; we could dine. I'll be back on Monday morning.'

'Enjoy your weekend, Helene.'

'Oh, I shall—although so much more if you were with me, Jules.'

He went home then, to take Bouncer for his last walk and then go to his study to work. It had been impossible to get Helene to listen to him, or to be serious about their future. He wondered if she had given serious thought to their marriage and the life they would lead together. She seemed unable to imagine any other way of life than a round of social pleasures. Somehow he must make her understand that her life would be utterly different from the one she now enjoyed, and then perhaps she might consider breaking off their engagement.

He drew the first of a pile of case-sheets towards him and began to read.

It was late on Sunday evening when he went to visit his mother.

'I thought you might bring Helene with you, Jules,' his mother observed. 'I haven't seen her since she was here, oh, some weeks ago, when Daisy was spending the day with me.'

'Helene has gone away for the weekend,' he told her. 'I saw her on Friday evening.'

'You haven't discussed the wedding yet?' persisted his mother gently.

'No. She has any number of social engagements, and I have a backlog of work.'

Katje came in with the coffee and Mevrouw der Huizma busied herself with the coffee tray. 'Did you see Daisy while you were in England, Jules?'

'Oh, yes.' He smiled suddenly. 'Mother, I can't talk about that—not yet! You don't mind?'

'No, dear. Now tell me about your work. That child with the dislocated hip you were so worried about—did you operate?'

'Yes—successfully, I'm glad to say. There's a small boy being admitted this week. I hope I shall be able to help him. Now tell me, how are the rest of the family?'

It was the middle of the week before he had a free evening. He phoned Helene. He would take her out to dinner somewhere quiet and they could talk…

Only Helene was going to a charity ball in Scheveningen. 'Something I can't cancel. It's a big event—two of the princes will be there. I simply can't miss it. Phone me later this week—perhaps we could spend Sunday together?'

He put the phone down and looked through his appointments book. He should have a free afternoon on Friday; he would go and see her then. There was a good chance that she would be at home; she had mentioned that she was going to the theatre in the evening so she would probably spend a quiet afternoon.

Helene was out when he arrived, soon after three o'clock. The maid who admitted him wasn't sure when she would be back, but if he cared to wait?

Mr der Huizma went to the drawing room and made himself comfortable in an oversized wing chair, refused the proffered tea or coffee and allowed his thoughts to wander; Daisy would be in the shop, wearing her serviceable dress, her hair very neat, no doubt selling some trifle to a customer or cleaning and polishing some small treasure which had come into her father's hands…

Half an hour later Helene returned home, bringing Hank with her. She spoke sharply to the maid as she entered the apartment and the woman, chivvied or ignored as the case might be, saw her chance for revenge. She said nothing to Helene about Mr der Huizma's presence in the drawing room.

He heard Helene's voice and Hank's laughter before they opened the door. Helene was speaking. 'Darling Hank, of course I'm going to marry him. He's got everything I want: money, the right ancestors, a brilliant career, and so engrossed in his work that I'll be free to do exactly as I want. We shall be able to go on seeing each other as often as we please. I shall have the best of both worlds…'

Mr der Huizma got out of his chair; a large man, he looked even larger now. He said mildly, 'I'm afraid I must disappoint you, Helene. You may have one world to your liking, but I'm afraid the second one won't be available.'

Helene had gone white. 'Jules, why wasn't I told that you were here? I was joking.' She turned to Hank. 'It was a joke, wasn't it, Hank?'

'Well, now, I rarely disagree with a lady, Helene, but it seemed to me that you meant every word. Mind you, Jules here might be prepared to overlook it, but somehow I don't think so. And I may not have any ancestors worth mentioning, but I've a nice place in California, as you know—and money.'

Mr der Huizma walked to the door. 'It does sound eminently satisfactory. I'm sure you're happy to release me from our engagement, Helene. I wish you both a happy future.'

He paused at the door. 'I will send an announcement to the papers. My regards to your mother and father.'

The maid, opening the door to him, wondered why he was smiling to himself. A nice, kind man, who deserved better than Juffrouw van Tromp. He bade her good day and got into his car and drove away to his home, where he ate a splendid tea, took Bouncer for a walk and then sat down at his desk to rearrange his schedule so that he could be free to go to England as soon as possible.

CHAPTER NINE

DAISY had gone to Exeter for an interview with one of the directors of a well-known firm of antique dealers there. They had an auction room and a quite large staff. If she accepted their offer she would start in a lowly way, cleaning pictures and silver, widening her knowledge of the antique trade. She had taken the morning bus and, with time on her hands, gone window shopping. The windows were full of clothes for summer—such pretty clothes—some of them affordable. But she went out so seldom they would hang in the wardrobe until they were last year's models.

It was a pity, she reflected, that when Jules had come she had been wearing an old skirt and cotton blouse. True, she had been able to wear the jersey dress on their day out together. But that was a year old and not this season's colour... She bought a lipstick under the eyes of a rather young lady on the other side of the counter, and searched for her mother's favourite soap—violet, in a pretty box with ribbons. She had a cup of coffee and a sandwich, spent half an hour wandering round the cathedral, and exactly on time presented herself at the antique dealers.

She was interviewed by a youngish man who made it obvious from the start that her chances of getting the job were small. He sat back in his chair behind the enormous desk, listening to Daisy's matter-of-fact recital of her experience. Which, he had to admit to himself, was adequate for the job. But the girl was too reserved. Too quiet...

He cut her short rather rudely, told her that he would let her know and thanked her in a perfunctory manner. Nor did he bother to get up as she got out of her chair. At the door she turned to look at him.

'I wouldn't like to work for you,' she told him politely, 'You have no manners.'

She closed the door behind her, leaving him with his mouth open.

She would have to wait until the five o'clock bus to go home; she went to the tea rooms in the cathedral close and ordered a pot of tea and scones. Her trip to Exeter had been a waste of time and money, and she knew that her father would be disappointed. She would have to think of something...

But she had no need to do that; there was a letter for her when she got home. She didn't open it at once, but gave her father an accurate account of her interview. 'Of course I shan't be offered the job,' she told him. 'I'm sorry, Father, but there are plenty of other opportunities...'

She opened her letter then, and read it, and read

it again before she said, 'It's from Janet—' the only cousin she had, daughter of her father's brother, and married with two children '—she wants me to go and stay for a week or two. Jack has been sent abroad by his firm, both children have the chicken-pox and she isn't well.'

She looked at her mother, who nodded her head silently. 'Of course you must go, dear. Poor Janet. Your father can get someone in to help for a week or two.' As he grumbled an answer she went on, 'There's Mrs Coffin—utterly reliable even if she can't sell anything. She can keep the shop open and do the odd jobs.' Mrs Gillard added in a wheedling tone, 'It's only for a week or two, dear.'

So Daisy packed a bag and took the bus to Totnes and walked up the hilly high street, under the arch, and turned down a narrow road leading away from it. Janet and Jack lived in a nice old house in a row of similar houses; they had been built more than a century ago and stood, solid and secure, lining the road going downhill. There were no front gardens, but they each had a long garden at the back, backing onto open country.

Daisy thumped the door knocker and opened the door, calling, 'It's me…'

Janet came running down the narrow stairs. 'Oh, Daisy, you angel. I hated having to ask you but there's no one else. I've friends, of course, but none of their children have had chickenpox so I couldn't ask them.' She asked anxiously, 'You have?'

'Yes, ages ago. They're in bed? And you? You look as though you should be in bed too.' Daisy put down her bag and took off her jacket. 'Well, now I'm here you can do just that, Janet. Just tell me if you need any shopping—and does the doctor call?'

'There's enough in the house for today. The doctor said he'd call this afternoon.'

'Good, so he can take a look at you at the same time as the children. I'll bring you a cup of tea when you're in bed, and see to James and Lucy.'

Janet in bed, and drinking her tea, Daisy went to look at the children. They were small, hot and cross, and very grizzly. She washed their little tear-stained faces, made their beds and found clean nightclothes, and went to inspect the fridge. There was plenty of ice cream; she spooned it into two small mouths and saw with satisfaction that they were dozing off.

It gave her time to take her bag to the small bedroom at the back of the house and then get a belated lunch for Janet and herself.

The doctor came later in the afternoon, pronounced the children progressing in the normal fashion, recommended that they stay in their beds for another day at least, and then went to take a look at Janet.

'Flu,' he diagnosed. 'Not severe, nothing that a

few days of paracetemol and plenty of fluids won't cure.' He observed that he was glad that Janet had help, and bade her good day. He would call again in two days' time, but if she was worried she could ring him at any time.

Daisy doled out the pills, saw to the children, got supper and took a tray up to Janet. And, since everyone seemed comfortable and disposed to settle down for the night, went to bed herself. She had phoned her mother, had had a phone call from Jack, anxious for news, and there was nothing more to be done until the next day.

The next few days went quickly seeing to the invalids, the housework, the shopping, the washing, and cooking the kind of food needed to tempt poor appetites kept Daisy busy. It was hard work but she didn't mind; the more she had to do the less time she had to think about Jules.

All the same, at bedtime, when there was nothing else to be done but get into bed and go to sleep, she allowed her thoughts free rein, going over every moment of their day together and his kiss. She had never meant to let him see how she felt when they had said goodbye; she would regret that for as long as she lived. Although it didn't matter now that they wouldn't see each other again. She wondered what he was doing, picturing him with Helene, dining and dancing or at the theatre. And Helene would be more beautiful than ever, and most certainly wearing the diamond brooch...

Her reflections, although vivid, were quite inaccurate. Mr der Huizma was at that very moment making his final preparations to travel to England.

Janet was back on her feet, rather pale and wan, and the children had been allowed out of their beds, which meant that they needed amusing for a large part of the day. Daisy, although she loved them dearly, couldn't help wishing that they could have had a few more days in the beds. Their spots were fading and they were more cheerful now, and beginning to eat their meals, but their increasing liveliness made Janet's head ache, so that she spent a good deal of time on her bed. Shopping was difficult, because it meant rousing Janet to look after the children while she was out, and there was always a small mountain of washing and ironing waiting.

It had been a trying morning. Lucy had been sick and James had flung his breakfast onto the floor; Janet had crept back to bed with a splitting headache. Daisy, mopping up and wiping tearful little faces, hoped that the day would improve. And certainly there was a bright spot—Jack phoned to say that he would be home in two days' time. Daisy assured him that all was well, settled the children with their toys, took a cup of coffee up to Janet and went to inspect the fridge. Scrambled eggs for lunch, she decided, and there was enough ice cream for the little ones. If Janet felt better later in the day she could go out to the shops…

She took a tray up to Janet presently, and then sat down at the kitchen table with James in his high chair and Lucy on her knee, spooning in the scrambled egg. They would have their afternoon nap presently, and she would make herself a pot of tea and some toast.

She frowned as the front door knocker was thumped in a no-nonsense manner. The milkman had been, and so had the postman; it would be someone wanting to read the meter or sell her some dishcloths. She ignored it, and popped another spoonful of egg into a small pink mouth. But whoever it was wasn't going to take no for an answer.

She hoisted Lucy onto her shoulder, bade James be a good boy for just a minute and went to the door.

Mr der Huizma stood there, large and relaxed.

Daisy heaved Lucy into a more comfortable position. She said in a disbelieving voice, 'How did you get here?'

He looked down at her; anything he had intended to say to her was obviously something which must wait. He said, in a voice which held reassurance and a certainty that he was there to help, 'Hullo, Daisy,' and took Lucy from her. 'May I come in?'

'We're having lunch—scrambled eggs,' said Daisy. 'If you don't mind…'

He walked past her into the kitchen, sat down at the table, arranged Lucy comfortably on his knee and began to spoon egg into her mouth.

'Well,' said Daisy astonished.

'You forget,' he said smoothly, 'that I am a children's doctor.'

Janet's voice from upstairs wanted to know who it was. Daisy said, 'I'd better go and tell her,' then added, 'She's my cousin. Her husband isn't coming back until the day after tomorrow—she's been ill and the children have had chickenpox.'

'Ah—a family crisis; they do occur. Have you had your lunch?'

'Me? No. I'll have something later.' She blushed. 'I will make you some scrambled eggs and a cup of coffee if you don't mind waiting until I've put these two down for their nap.'

He said matter-of-factly, 'Go and tell your cousin that I'm here, and then see to these two. I'll go and get us something to eat and you can tell me how I can help.' When she hesitated, he said, 'No, don't argue, dear girl.'

So she went upstairs and told Janet, who watched Daisy's face as she talked and drew her own conclusions. 'How kind,' she commented. 'You could do with some help. If he likes to stay for tea I'll crawl down and meet him.'

And when Daisy went downstairs Mr der Huizma went quietly out of the house; by the time she got downstairs again, after putting the children down for a nap, it was to find that he was back, the table cleared and set with knives and forks and plates, one of the local butcher's famous pork pies on a dish and a bowl of salad beside it. There was a bottle of wine too.

'Come and sit down and tell me about it,' he invited. 'I hope your cousin doesn't find me a nuisance.'

Daisy eyed the pork pie. 'She says she'll come down to meet you if you would like to stay to tea.'

'Good. This isn't much of a meal, but if you're hungry…'

'Oh, but I am,' said Daisy and fell to!

Mr der Huizma resisted a strong desire to snatch her off her chair and carry her off somewhere quiet and tell her that he loved her, but he could see that his desires must take second place to the pork pie. His darling Daisy had obviously not been eating enough to keep a mouse alive…

He poured her a glass of wine and said soothingly, 'Drink this; it's a very light wine, just right for the pie.'

And when they had eaten he helped her clear the table and then washed up.

Daisy, drying plates, said, 'I'm sure you never wash up at home.'

'No, but I know how to do it.' He emptied the water away, wiped the sink tidily and hung up the teatowel. 'Now, let us sit down and see if we can improve this situation.'

'Well,' began Daisy, 'you're very kind, but shouldn't you be with your friends? Where you stay when you come down here?'

'I shall return there this evening, but in the meantime may I suggest that I do any necessary shopping for you? There is nothing much in the fridge, is there?'

She looked at him doubtfully. 'I can't think why you're here. How did you know?'

'I called on your mother and father. Let us keep to the point. What do these toddlers eat other than scrambled egg? Make a list and I'll fetch whatever you need.'

'Now?'

'Now, Daisy. And when I come back perhaps your cousin will feel well enough to come downstairs and we can have a cup of tea together.'

She had the feeling that he was taking over the household whether she liked it or not. Upon reflection she decided that she liked it. She sat down and made a list.

'You're very kind. I'll give you some money...'

'No, no. We can settle up later.'

When he had gone she went upstairs and explained to Janet, who declared that she felt better and was all agog to hear what Daisy had to say.

'You mean to say,' she said, when Daisy had given her a brief resumé of her visitor, 'that he's come over here to see you?'

'No, of course not. He comes to England quite often to the London hospitals. I told you he had met Mother and Father; I dare say they mentioned that I was staying here and he's just called on his way to somewhere or other.'

'Well, when he is back and tea's ready, I'll come down,' said Janet. 'And I'll see to Lucy and Jamie when they wake.'

He'd be gone for an hour at least, decided Daisy, and got out the ironing board.

Unlike the average housewife, going from shop to shop with an eye on the household purse, Mr der Huizma had walked into the nearest grocer's and asked for everything necessary to keep a small household with two children supplied with suitable food. 'Enough for two or three days,' he'd added.

Janet had come downstairs and was there to open the door to his knock. He introduced himself and was led into the kitchen, where Daisy stood ironing diminutive garments. She looked up as he went in.

'I'm going to make tea as soon as I've finished this...'

He put his carrier bags down on the table. 'I dare say you'd like to put these things away?' he asked Janet. 'And I'd love a cup of tea when Daisy's finished.'

Daisy went on ironing, listening to him and Janet chatting as they stowed the food away, and then the children woke up and Janet went to bring them downstairs.

'I'll put the kettle on,' said Mr der Huizma.

'You're very domesticated,' said Daisy tartly. She was tired, and he was behaving like a big brother or an uncle or someone equally dull.

'Only when I am obliged to be! You're cross, aren't you? Tired too. There's a steak pie in the fridge; it only needs to be warmed up. And a milk pudding for the children. Go to bed early, Daisy.'

Janet came down with the children then, and he sat down with them on his knee until Janet had made tea. Daisy, ironing the last nightdress, could see that he was quite at ease with them. She supposed that he had plenty of practice on his wards...

After tea he got up to go, waving away Janet's thanks. At the door he said, 'I'll fetch you tomorrow evening, Daisy. I have to go to Plymouth in the morning but I should be here around six o'clock.'

'I won't…' began Daisy.

'Yes, you will!' he assured her, and smiled so that her heart missed a beat.

When he had gone, Daisy said, 'I was going to stay until Jack got here. Can you manage, Janet?'

'Of course I can. I'm feeling quite well again, and the children are themselves once more. Jack will be home in the morning and I'll have everything ready for him. You've been an angel and that Mr der Huizma of yours is marvellous. Are you sure he isn't in love with you, Daisy?'

'Well, perhaps he is a bit, but he's going to marry someone in Holland.'

'Holland's a long way off and you're here,' said Janet. 'Now, let's get supper and go through the fridge. He wouldn't let me pay for anything, said it was a small return for accepting him as a friend…'

Daisy was ready when he arrived the following evening. He had flowers for Janet and a soft woolly toy for each of the children, and when Janet invited him to come and see them any time he was in England, he accepted with the charming good manners which came naturally to him. He had greeted Daisy with a casual friendliness which lasted for their journey back to her home. He didn't talk much, and when he did it was about impersonal matters, and Daisy, facing another goodbye, was in no mood to make polite conversation. When they reached her home he went in with her and spent a short time talking to her mother and father. Going to the door with him at last, Daisy offered a hand. Another goodbye, she thought unhappily, and this must really be the last one. Perhaps he would kiss her...

He didn't. He shook her hand briefly and got back into his car. Daisy went back to the living room and gave her mother and father a long and elaborate account of her stay with Janet, making light of Mr der Huizma's visit.

Her mother, listening to her bright chatter, said presently, 'Well, darling, you've earned a day or two's holiday. Mrs Coffin is coming in for the rest of this week so you can do whatever you want to do.'

Daisy cried herself to sleep and woke early. She couldn't think of anything she wanted to do; she would potter around at home, helping her mother and doing the shopping. She didn't want to go near the beach. To see Jules again didn't bear thinking of.

She collected her basket and her mother's shopping list after breakfast and set off for Pati's supermarket up by the church. It wasn't really a supermarket but Mr Pati, hard-working and a good businessman, liked to keep up with the times, and although it was small, it was an exact model of the vast supermarkets in Plymouth and Exeter.

It was still early, and there were no customers. Daisy asked after his wife's asthma, his small son's tonsils and his own aches and pains, which all took some time, but since time was something to pass as quickly as possible that didn't matter. Presently she took a trolley and got out her list.

She was reaching for Assam tea, always on the top shelf and almost out of reach, when a large hand lifted it down.

'One or two?' asked Mr der Huizma.

Daisy turned to face him. It really was too much. Why couldn't he just go away? She voiced the thought out loud.

'I came to England—and it was most inconvenient too—to talk to you, Daisy. That was impossible at Totnes, so I am reduced to going shopping with you.'

Daisy put two tins of Italian chopped tomatoes into the trolley. 'Well, whatever it is you want to talk about, we can't do it here.'

'Oh, but we can! It is hardly the ideal surroundings, but I haven't the time to look for a suitably romantic background.'

He tossed two tins of asparagus tips into the trolley, and then added a packet of ravioli. Daisy reached for a jar of coffee and he, not to be outdone, added three tins of cat food.

'We haven't got a cat,' said Daisy.

'Then we will take it back with us; Jette has a cat and kittens.'

They were going slowly along the shelves, the list forgotten, although from time to time Mr der Huizma added some item or other to the growing pile in the trolley. At the end of the narrow aisle he put a hand over hers on the trolley handle.

'My darling girl, will you stand still just long enough for me to tell you that I love you? I've come all this way just to tell you that.'

Daisy looked at him. 'Helene,' she said in a sad voice.

'Helene has broken our engagement; she will eventually, I believe, go to California with someone called Hank.'

'You loved her…?'

'No. I may have been a little in love with her when we were first engaged. And then, when I saw you walking along the shore—you have been in my heart and my head ever since, my dear love. And I thought I had no chance with you, and then, that last time when we said goodbye, and you said, "Jules," in such a loving, unhappy voice… Will you marry me, Daisy? And learn to love me as much as I love you?'

'Oh, Jules,' said Daisy, an entirely satisfactory answer which swept her into his arms to be kissed and kissed again. Presently, when she had her breath back, she said, 'Yes, I'll marry you, Jules, of course I will. I've loved you for weeks.'

He kissed her again, and Mr Pati, watching from a discreet distance, crept a bit closer and stealthily wheeled the trolley back to the check-out desk. He was a romantic man at heart, and he liked Daisy, but business was business, so he began to tot up the goods in the trolley. A most satisfactory start to the day.